Masterpieces Of American Wit And Humor

Thomas L. Masson

Contents

MASTERPIECES
OF AMERICAN
WIT AND HUMOR

BY

Thomas L. Masson

Agnes Repplier
A PLEA FOR HUMOR

More than half a dozen years have passed since Mr. Andrew Lang, startled for once out of his customary light-heartedness, asked himself, and his readers, and the ghost of Charles Dickens--all three powerless to answer--whether the dismal seriousness of the present day was going to last forever; or whether, when the great wave of earnestness had rippled over our heads, we would pluck up heart to be merry and, if needs be, foolish once again. Not that mirth and folly are in any degree synonymous, as of old; for the merry fool, too scarce, alas! even in the times when Jacke of Dover hunted for him in the highways, has since then grown to be rarer than a phenix. He has carried his cap and bells and jests and laughter elsewhere, and has left us to the mercies of the serious fool, who is by no means so seductive a companion. If the Cocquecigrues are in possession of the land, and if they are tenants exceedingly hard to evict, it is because of the encouragement they receive from those to whom we innocently turn for help: from the poets, novelists and men of letters whose duty it is to brighten and make glad our days.

"It is obvious," sighs Mr. Birrell dejectedly, "that many people appear to like a drab-colored world, hung around with dusky shreds of philosophy"; but it is more obvious still that, whether they like it or not, the drapings grow a trifle dingier every year, and that no one seems to have the courage to tack up something gay. What is much worse, even those bits of wanton color which have rested generations of weary eyes are being rapidly obscured by somber and intricate scroll-work, warranted to oppress and fatigue. The great masterpieces of humor, which have kept men young by laughter, are being tried in the courts of an orthodox morality and found lamentably wanting; or else, by way of giving them another chance, they

are being subjected to the *peine forte et dure* of modern analysis, and are revealing hideous and melancholy meanings in the process. I have always believed that
Hudibras owes its chilly treatment at the hands of critics--with the single and most
genial exception of Sainte-Beuve--to the absolute impossibility of twisting it into
something serious. Strive as we may, we cannot put a new construction on those
vigorous old jokes, and to be simply and barefacedly amusing is no longer considered a sufficient *raison d'etre*. It is the most significant token of our ever- increas-
ing "sense of moral responsibility in literature" that we should be always trying to
graft our own conscientious purposes upon those authors who, happily for themselves, lived and died before virtue, colliding desperately with cakes and ale, had
imposed such depressing obligations.

   "'Don Quixote,'" says Mr. Shorthouse with unctuous gravity, "will come in time
to be recognized as one of the saddest books ever written"; and, if the critics keep
on expounding it much longer, I truly fear it will. It may be urged that Cervantes
himself was low enough to think it exceedingly funny; but then one advantage of
our new and keener insight into literature is to prove to us how indifferently great
authors understood their own masterpieces. Shakespeare, we are told, knew comparatively little about "Hamlet," and he is to be congratulated on his limitations.
Defoe would hardly recognize "Robinson Crusoe" as "a picture of civilization," having innocently supposed it to be quite the reverse; and he would be as amazed as
we are to learn from Mr. Frederic Harrison that his book contains "more psychology, more political economy, and more anthropology than are to be found in many
elaborate treatises on these especial subjects"--blighting words which I would not
even venture to quote if I thought that any boy would chance to read them and so
have one of the pleasures of his young life destroyed. As for "Don Quixote," which
its author persisted in regarding with such misplaced levity, it has passed through
many bewildering vicissitudes. It has figured bravely as a satire on the Duke of
Lerma, on Charles V., on Philip II., on Ignatius Loyola-Cervantes was the most
devout of Catholics--and on the Inquisition, which, fortunately, did not think so.
In fact, there is little or nothing which it has not meant in its time; and now, having attained that deep spiritual inwardness which we have been recently told is
lacking in poor Goldsmith, we are requested by Mr. Shorthouse to refrain from all
brutal laughter, but, with a shadowy smile and a profound seriousness, to attune

ourselves to the proper state of receptivity. Old-fashioned, coarse-minded people may perhaps ask, "But if we are not to laugh at 'Don Quixote,' at whom are we, please, to laugh?"--a question which I, for one, would hardly dare to answer. Only, after r eading the following curious sentence, extracted from a lately published volume of criticism, I confess to finding myself in a state of mental perplexity utterly alien to mirth. "How much happier," its author sternly reminds us, "was poor Don Quixote in his energetic career, in his earnest redress of wrong, and in his ultimate triumph over self, than he could have been in the gnawing reproach and spiritual stigma which a yielding to weakness never failingly entails!" Beyond this point it would be hard to go. Were these things really spoken of the "ingenious gentleman" of La Mancha or of John Howard or George Peabody or perhaps Elizabeth Fry--or is there no longer such a thing as recognized absurdity In the world?

Another gloomy indication of the departure of humor from our midst is the tendency of philosophical writers to prove by analysis that, if they are not familiar with the thing itself, they at least know of what it should consist. Mr. Shorthouse's depressing views about "Don Quixote" are merely introduced as illustrating a very scholarly and comfortless paper on the subtle qualities of mirth. No one could deal more gracefully and less humorously with his topic than does Mr. Shorthouse, and we are compelled to pause every now and then and reassure ourselves as to the subject matter of his eloquence. Professor Everett has more recently and more cheerfully defined for us the Philosophy of the Comic, in a way which, if it does not add to our gaiety, cannot be accused of plunging us deliberately into gloom. He thinks, indeed--and small wonder--that there is "a genuine difficulty in distinguishing between the comic and the tragic," and that what we need is some formula which shall accurately interpret the precise qualities of each, and he is disposed to illustrate his theory by dwelling on the tragic side of Falstaff, which is, of all injuries, the grimmest and hardest to forgive. Falstaff is now the forlorn hope of those who love to laugh, and when he is taken away from us, as soon, alas! he will be, and sleeps with Don Quixote in the "dull cold marble" of an orthodox sobriety, how shall we make merry our souls? Mr. George Radford, who enriched the first volume of "Obiter dicta" with such a loving study of the fat-witted old knight, tells us reassuringly that by laughter man is distinguished from the beasts, though the cares and sorrows of life have all but deprived him of this elevating grace and degraded him into a brutal solemnity. Then comes along a rare genius like Falstaff, who restores the power of laughter, and transforms the stolid brute once more into a man, and who accordingly has the highest claim to our grateful and affectionate regard. That there are those who persist in looking upon him as a selfish and worthless fellow is, from Mr. Radford's point of view, a sorrowful instance of human thanklessness and perversity. But this I take to be the enamored and exaggerated language of a too faithful partizan. Morally speaking, Falstaff has not a leg to stand upon, and there is a tragic element lurking always amid the fun. But, seen in the broad sunlight of his transcendent humor, this shadow is as the halfpennyworth of bread to his own noble ocean of sack, and why should we be forever trying to force it into prominence? When Charlotte Bronte advised her friend Ellen Nussey to read none of Shakespeare's comedies, she was not beguiled for a moment into regarding them as serious and melancholy lessons of life; but with uncompromising directness put them down as mere improper plays, the amusing qualities of which were insufficient to excuse their coarseness, and which were manifestly unfit for the "gentle Ellen's" eyes.

In fact, humor would at all times have been the poorest excuse to offer to Miss Bronte for any form of moral dereliction, for it was the one quality she lacked herself and failed to tolerate in others. Sam Weller was apparently as obnoxious to her as was Falstaff, for she would not even consent to meet Dickens when she was being lionized in London society--a degree of abstemiousness on her part which it is disheartening to contemplate. It does not seem too much to say that every shortcoming in Charlotte Bronte's admirable work, every limitation in her splendid genius, arose primarily from her want of humor. Her severities of judgment--and who more severe than she?--were due to the same melancholy cause; for humor is the kindliest thing alive. Compare the harshness with which she handles her hapless curates and the comparative crudity of her treatment, with the surprising lightness of Miss Austen's touch as she rounds and completes her immortal clerical portraits. Miss Bronte tells us, in one of her letters, that she regarded *all* curates as "highly uninteresting, narrow, and unattractive specimens of the coarser sex," just as she found *all* the Belgian schoolgirls "cold, selfish, animal and inferior." But to Miss Austen's keen and friendly eye the narrowest of clergymen was not wholly uninteresting, the most inferior of schoolgirls not without some claim to our consideration; even the coarseness of the male sex was far from vexing her maidenly serenity, probably because she was unacquainted with the Rochester type. Mr. Elton is certainly narrow, Mary Bennet extremely inferior; but their authoress only laughs at them softly, with a quiet tolerance and a good-natured sense of amusement at their follies. It was little wonder that Charlotte Bronte, who had at all times the courage of her convictions, could not and would not read Jane Austen's novels. "They have not got story enough for me," she boldly affirmed. "I don't want my blood curdled, but I like to have it stirred. Miss Austen strikes me as milk-and-watery and, to say truth, dull." Of course she did! How was a woman, whose ideas of after-dinner conversation are embodied in the amazing language of Baroness Ingram and her titled friends to appreciate the delicious, sleepy small-talk in "Sense and Sensibility," about the respective heights of the respective grandchildren? It is to Miss Bronte's abiding lack of humor that we owe such stately caricatures as Blanche Ingram and all the high-born, ill-bred company who gather in Thornfield Hall, like a group fresh from Madame Tussaud's ingenious workshop, and against whose waxen unreality Jane Eyre and Rochester, alive to their very finger-tips, contrast like twin sparks of fire. It was her lack of humor, too, which beguiled her into asserting that the forty "wicked, sophistical and immoral French novels" which found their way down to lonely Haworth gave her "a thorough idea of France and Paris"--alas! poor, misjudged France!--and which made her think Thackeray very nearly as wicked, sophistical and immoral as the French novels. Even her dislike for children was probably due to the same irremediable misfortune; for the humors of children are the only redeeming points amid their general naughtiness and vexing misbehavior. Mr. Swinburne, guiltless himself of any jocose tendencies, has made the unique discovery that Charlotte Bronte strongly resembles Cervantes, and that Paul Emanuel is a modern counterpart of Don Quixote; and well it is for our poet that the irascible little professor never heard him hint at such a similarity. Surely, to use one of Mr. Swinburne's own incomparable expressions, the parallel is no better than a "subsimious absurdity."

On the other hand, we are told that Miss Austen owed her lively sense of humor to her habit of dissociating the follies of mankind from any rigid standard of right and wrong; which means, I suppose, that she never dreamed she had a mission. Nowadays, indeed, no writer is without one. We cannot even read a paper upon gypsies and not become aware that its author is deeply imbued with a sense of his personal responsibility for these agreeable rascals whom he insists upon our taking seriously as if we wanted to have anything to do with them on such terms! "Since the time of Carlyle," says Mr. Bagehot, "earnestness has been a favorite virtue in literature"; but Oarlyle, though sharing largely in that profound melancholy which he declared to be the basis of every English soul, and though he was unfortunate enough to think Pickwick sad trash, had nevertheless a grim and eloquent humor of his own. With him, at least, earnestness never degenerated into dulness; and while dulness may be, as he unhesitatingly affirmed, the first requisite for a great and free people, yet a too heavy percentage of this valuable quality is fatal to the sprightly grace of literature. "In our times," said an old Scotchwoman, "there's fully mony modern principles," and the first of these seems to be the substitution of a serious and critical discernment for the light-hearted sympathy of former days. Our grandfathers cried a little and laughed a good deal over their books, without the smallest sense of anxiety or responsibility in the matter; but we are called on repeatedly to face problems which we would rather let alone, to dive dismally into motives, to trace subtle connections, to analyze uncomfortable sensations, and to exercise in all cases a discreet and conscientious severity, when what we really want and need is half an hour's amusement. There is no stronger proof of the great change that has swept over mankind than the sight of a nation which used to chuckle over "Tom Jones" absorbing a few years ago countless editions of "Robert Elsmer e." What is droller still is that the people who read "Robert Elsmere" would think it wrong to enjoy "Tom Jones," and that the people who enjoyed "Tom Jones" would have thought it wrong to read "Robert Elsmere"; and that the people who, wishing to be on the safe side of virtue, think it wrong to read either, are scorned greatly as lacking true moral discrimination.

Now he would be a brave man who would undertake to defend the utterly indefensible literature of the past. Where it was most humorous it was also most coarse, wanton and cruel; but, in banishing these objectionable qualities, we have effectually contrived to rid ourselves of the humor as well, and with it we have lost one of the safest instincts of our souls. Any book which serves to lower the sum of human gaiety is a moral delinquent; and instead of coddling it into universal notice and growing owlish in its gloom, we should put it briskly aside in favor of brighter and pleasanter things. When Father Faber said that there was no greater help to a religious life than a keen sense of the ridiculous, he startled a number of pious people, yet what a luminous and cordial message it was to help us on our way! Mr. Birrell has recorded the extraordinary delight with which he came across some after-dinner sally of the Reverend Henry Martyn's; for the very thought of that ardent and fiery spirit relaxing into pleasantries over the nuts and wine made him appear like an actual fellow-being of our own. It is with the same feeling intensified, as I have already noted, that we read some of the letters of the early fathers--those grave and hallowed figures seen through a mist of centuries--and find them jesting at one another in the gayest and least sacerdotal manner imaginable. "Who could tell a story with more wit, who could joke so pleasantly?" sighs St. Gregory of Nazienzen of his friend St. Basil, remembering doubtless with a heavy heart the shafts of good-humored raillery that had brightened their lifelong intercourse. With what kindly and loving zest does Gregory, himself the most austere of men, mock at Basil's asceticism--at those "sad and hungry banquets" of which he was invited to partake, those "ungarden-like gardens, void of pot-herbs," in which he was expected to dig! With what delightful alacrity does Basil vindicate his reputation for humor by making a most excellent joke in court, for the benefit of a brutal magistrate who fiercely threatened to tear out his liver! "Your intention is a benevolent one," said the saint, who had been for years a confirmed invalid. "Where it is now located, it has given me nothing but trouble." Surely, as we read such an anecdote as this, we share in the curious sensation experienced by little Tom Tulliver, when, by dint of Maggie's repeated questions, he began slowly to understand that the Romance had once been real men, who were happy enough to speak their own language without any previous introduction to the Eton grammar. In like manner, when we come to realize that the fathers of the primitive church enjoyed their quips and cranks and jests as much as do Mr. Trollope's jolly deans or vicars, we feel we have at last grasped the secret of their identity, and we appreciate the force of Father Faber's appeal to the frank spirit of a wholesome mirth.

Perhaps one reason for the scanty tolerance that humor receives at the hands of the disaffected is because of the rather selfish way in which the initiated enjoy their fun; for there is always a secret irritation about a laugh in which we cannot join. Mr. George Saintsbury is plainly of this way of thinking, and, being blessed beyond his fellows with a love for all that is jovial, he speaks from out of the richness of his experience. "Those who have a sense of humor," he says, "instead of being quietly and humbly thankful, are perhaps a little too apt to celebrate their joy in the face of the afflicted ones who have it not; and the afflicted ones only follow a general law in protesting that it is a very worthless thing, if not a complete humbug." This spirit of exclusiveness on the one side and of irascibility on the other may be greatly deplored, but who is there among us, I wonder, wholly innocent of blame? Mr. Saintsbury himself confesses to a silent chuckle of delight when he thinks of the dimly veiled censoriousness with which Peacock's inimitable humor has been received by one-half of the reading world. In other words, his enjoyment of the Reverend Doctors Folliott and Opimian is sensibly increased by the reflection that a great many worthy people, even among his own acquaintances, are, by some mysterious law of their being, debarred from any share in his pleasure. Yet surely we need not be so niggardly in this matter. There is wit enough in those two reverend gentlemen to go all around the living earth and leave plenty for generations now unborn. Each might say with Juliet:

"The more I give to thee,
The more I have;"

for wit is as infinite as love, and a deal more lasting in its qualities. When Peacock describes a country gentleman's range of ideas as "nearly commensurate with that of the great king Nebuchadnezzar when he was turned out to grass," he affords us a happy illustration of the eternal fitness of humor, for there can hardly come a time when such an apt comparison will fail to point its meaning.

Mr. Birrell is quite as selfish in his felicity as Mr. Saintsbury, and perfectly frank in acknowledging it. He dwells rapturously over certain well-loved pages of "Pride and Prejudice" and "Mansfield Park," and then deliberately adds, "When an admirer of Miss Austen reads these familiar passages, the smile of satisfaction, betraying the deep inward peace they never fail to beget, widens like 'a circle in the water,' as he remembers (and he is always careful to remember) how his dearest friend, who has been so successful in life, can no more read Miss Austen than he can read the Moabitish stone." The same peculiarity is noticeable in the more ardent lovers of Charles Lamb. They seem to want him all to themselves, look askance upon any fellow-being who ventures to assert a modest preference for their idol, and brighten visibly when some ponderous critic declares the Letters to be sad stuff and not worth half the exasperating nonsense talked about them. Yet Lamb flung his good things to the wind with characteristic prodigality, little recking by whom or in what spirit they were received. How many witticisms, I wonder, were roared into the deaf ears of old Thomas Westwood, who heard them not, alas! but who laughed all the same, out of pure sociability, and with a pleasant sense that something funny had been said! And what of that ill-fated pun which Lamb, in a moment of deplorable abstraction, let fall at a funeral, to the surprise and consternation of the mourners? Surely a man who could joke at a funeral never meant his pleasantries to be hoarded up for the benefit of an initiated few, but would gladly see them the property of all living men; ay, and of all dead men, too, were such a distribution possible. "Damn the age! I will write for antiquity!" he exclaimed with not unnatural heat when the "Gypsy's Malison" was rejected by the ingenious editors of the *Gem*, on the ground that it would "shock all mothers"; and even this expression, uttered with pardonable irritation, manifests no solicitude for a narrow and esoteric audience.

"Wit is useful for everything, but sufficient for nothing," says Amiel, who probably felt he needed some excuse for burying so much of his Gallic sprightliness in Teutonic gloom; and dulness, it must be admitted, has the distinct advantage of being useful for everybody and sufficient for nearly everybody as well. Nothing, we are told, is more rational than ennui; and Mr. Bagehot, contemplating the "grave files of speechless men" who have always represented the English land, exults more openly and energetically even than Carlyle in the saving dulness, the superb impenetrability, which stamps the Englishman, as it stamped the Roman, with the sign-manual of patient strength. Stupidity, he reminds us, is not folly, and moreover it often insures a valuable consistency. "What I says is this here, as I was a-saying yesterday, is the average Englishman's notion of historical eloquence and habitual discretion." But Mr. Bagehot could well afford to trifle thus coyly with dulness, because he knew it only theoretically and as a dispassionate observer. His own roof-tree is free from the blighting presence; his own pages are guiltless of the leaden touch. It has been well said that an ordinary mortal might live for a twelvemonth like a gentleman on Hazlitt's ideas; but he might, if he were clever, shine all his life long with the reflected splendor of Mr. Bagehot's wit, and be thought to give forth a very respectable illumination. There is a telling quality in every stroke; a pitiless dexterity that drives the weapon, like a fairy's arrow, straight to some vital point. When we read that "of all pursuits ever invented by man for separating the faculty of argument from the capacity of belief, the art of debating is probably the most effective," we feel that an unwelcome statement has been expressed with Mephistophelian coolness; and remembering that these words were uttered before Mr. Gladstone had attained his parliamentary preeminence, we have but another proof of the imperishable accuracy of wit. Only say a clever thing, and mankind will go on forever furnishing living illustrations of its truth. It was Thurlow who originally remarked that, "companies have neither bodies to kick nor souls to lose," and the jest fits in so aptly with our everyday humors and experiences that I have heard men attribute it casually to their friends, thinking, perhaps, that it must have been born in these times of giant corporations, of city railroads, and of trusts. What a gap between Queen Victoria and Queen Bess; what a thorough and far-reaching change in everything that goes to make up the life and habits of men; and yet Shakespeare's fine strokes of humor have become so fitted to our common speech that the very unconsciousness with which we apply them proves how they tally with our modern emotions and opportunities. Lesser lights burn quite as steadily. Pope and Goldsmith reappear on the lips of people whose knowledge of the "Essay on Man" is of the very haziest character, and whose acquaintance with "She Stoops to Conquer" is confined exclusively to Mr. Abbey's graceful illustrations. Not very long ago I heard a bright schoolgirl, when reproached for wet feet or some such youthful indiscretion, excuse herself gaily on the plea that she was "bullying nature"; and, knowing that the child was but modestly addicted to her books, I wondered how many of Doctor Holmes's trenchant sayings have become a heritage in our households, detached often from their original kinship, and seeming like the rightful property of every one who utters them. It is an amusing, barefaced, witless sort of robbery, yet surely not without its compensations; for it must be a pleasant thing to reflect in old age that the general murkiness of life has been lit up here and there by sparks struck from one's youthful fire, and that these sparks, though they wander occasionally masterless as will-o'-the-wisps, are destined never to go out.

Are destined never to go out! In its vitality lies the supreme excellence of humor. Whatever has "wit enough to keep it sweet" defies corruption and outlasts all time; but the wit must be of that outward and visible order which needs no introduction or demonstration at our hands. It is an old trick with dull novelists to describe their characters as being exceptionally brilliant people, and to trust that we will take their word for it and ask no further proof. Every one remembers how Lord Beaconsfield would tell us that a cardinal could "sparkle with anecdote and blaze with repartee"; and how utterly destitute of sparkle or blaze were the specimens of His Eminence's conversation with which we were subsequently favored. Those "lively dinners" in "Endymion" and "Lothair" at which we were assured the brightest minds in England loved to gather became mere Barmecide feasts when reported to us without a single amusing remark, such waifs and strays of conversation as reached our ears being of the dreariest and most fatuous description. It is not so with the real masters of their craft. Mr. Peacock does not stop to explain to us that Doctor Folliott is witty. The reverend gentleman opens his mouth and acquaints us with the fact himself. There is no need for George Eliot to expatiate on Mrs. Poyser's humor. Five minutes of that lady's society is amply sufficient for the revelation. We do not even hear Mr. Poyser and the rest of the family enlarging delightedly on the subject, as do all of Lawyer Putney's friends, in Mr. Howells's story, "Annie Kilburn"; and yet even the united testimony of Hatboro' fails to clear up our lingering doubts concerning Mr. Putney's wit. The dull people of that soporific town are really and truly and realistically dull. There is no mistaking them. The stamp of veracity is upon every brow. They pay morning calls, and we listen to their conversation with a dreamy impression that we have heard it all many times before, and that the ghosts of our own morning calls are revisiting us, not in the glimpses of the moon, but in Mr. Howells's decorous and quiet pages. That curious conviction that we have formerly passed through a precisely similar experience is strong upon us as we read, and it is the most emphatic testimony to the novelist's peculiar skill. But there is none of this instantaneous acquiescence in Mr. Putney's wit; for although he does make one very nice little joke, it is hardly enough to flavor all his conversation, which is for the most part rather unwholesome than humorous. The only way to elucidate him is to suppose that Mr. Howells, in sardonic mood, wishes to show us that if a man be discreet enough to take to hard drinking in his youth, before his general emptiness is ascertained, his friends invariably credit him with a host of shining qualities which, we are given to understand he balked and frustrated by his one unfortunate weakness. How many of us know these exceptionally brilliant lawyers, doctors, politicians and journalists who bear a charmed reputation based exclusively upon their inebriety, and who take good care not to imperil it by too long a relapse into the mortifying self-revelations of soberness! And what wrong has been done to the honored name of humor by these pretentious rascals! We do not love Falstaff because he is drunk; we do not admire Becky Sharp because she is wicked. Drunkenness and wickedness are things easy of imitation; yet all the sack in Christendom could not beget us another Falstaff--though Seithenyn ap Seithyn comes very near to the incomparable model--and all the wickedness in the world could not fashion us a second Becky Sharp. There are too many dull topers and stupid sinners among mankind to admit of any uncertainty on these points.

Bishop Burnet, in describing Lord Halifax, tells us, with thinly veiled disapprobation, that he was "a man of fine and ready wit, full of life, and very pleasant, but much turned to satire. His imagination was too hard for his judgment, and a severe jest took more with him than all arguments whatever." Yet this was the first statesman of his age, and one whose clear and tranquil vision penetrated so far beyond the turbulent, troubled times he lived in that men looked askance upon a power they but dimly understood. The sturdy "Trimmer," who would be bullied neither by king nor commons, who would "speak his mind and not be hanged as long as there was law in England," must have turned with infinite relief from the horrible medley of plots and counterplots, from the ugly images of Oates and Dangerfield, from the scaffolds of Stafford and Russell and Sidney, from the Bloody Circuit and the massacre of Glencoe, from the false smiles of princes and the howling arrogance of the mob, to any jest, however "severe," which would restore to him his cold and fastidious serenity and keep his judgment and his good temper unimpaired. "Ridicule is the test of truth," said Hazlitt, and it is a test which Halifax remorselessly applied, and which would not be without its uses to the Trimmer of to-day, in whom this adjusting sense is lamentably lacking. For humor distorts nothing, and only false gods are laughed off their earthly pedestals. What monstrous absurdities and paradoxes have resisted whole batteries of serious arguments, and then crumbled swiftly into dust before the ringing death-knell of a laugh! What healthy exultation, what genial mirth, what loyal brotherhood of mirth attends the friendly sound! Yet in labeling our life and literature, as the Danes labeled their Royal Theatre in Copenhagen, "Not for amusement merely," we have pushed one step further, and the legend too often stands, "Not for amusement at all." Life is no laughing matter, we are told, which is true; and, what is still more dismal to contemplate, books are no laughing matters, either. Only now and then some gay, defiant rebel, like Mr. Saintsbury, flaunts the old flag, hums a bar of "Blue Bonnets over the Border," and ruffles the quiet waters of our souls by hinting that this age of Apollinaris and of lectures is at fault, and that it has produced nothing which can vie as literature with the products of the ages of wine and song.

Marietta Holley
AN UNMARRIED FEMALE

I suppose we are about as happy as the most of folks, but as I was sayin' a few days ago to Betsey Bobbet, a neighborin' female of ours--"Every station-house in life has its various skeletons. But we ort to try to be contented with that spear of life we are called on to handle." Betsey hain't married, and she don't seem to be contented. She is awful opposed to wimmin's rights--she thinks it is wimmin's only spear to marry, but as yet she can't find any man willin' to lay holt of that spear with her. But you can read in her daily life, and on her eager, willin' countenance, that she fully realizes the sweet words of the poet, "While there is life there is hope."

Betsey hain't handsome. Her cheek-bones are high, and she bein' not much more than skin and bone they show plainer than they would if she was in good order. Her complexion (not that I blame her for it) hain't good, and her eyes are little and sot way back in her head. Time has seen fit to deprive her of her hair and teeth, but her large nose he has kindly suffered her to keep, but she has got the best white ivory teeth money will buy, and two long curls fastened behind each ear, besides frizzles on the top of her head; and if she wasn't naturally bald, and if the curls was the color of her hair, they would look well. She is awful sentimental; I have seen a good many that had it bad, but of all the sentimental creeters I ever did see, Betsey Bobbet is the sentimentalest; you couldn't squeeze a laugh out of her with a cheeze-press.

As I said, she is awful opposed to wimmin's havin' any right, only the right to get married. She holds on to that right as tight as any single woman I ever see, which makes it hard and wearyin' on the single men round here.

For take the men that are the most opposed to wimmin's havin' a right, and talk the most about its bein' her duty to cling to man like a vine to a tree, they don't want Betsey to cling to them; they won't let her cling to 'em. For when they would be a-goin' on about how wicked it was for wimmin to vote--and it was her only spear to marry, says I to 'em, "Which had you ruther do, let Betsey Bobbet cling to you or let her vote?" and they would every one of 'em quail before that question. They would drop their heads before my keen gray eyes--and move off the subject.

But Betsey don't get discouraged. Every time I see her she says in a hopeful, wishful tone, "That the deepest men of minds in the country agree with her in thinkin' that it is wimmin's duty to marry and not to vote." And then she talks a sight about the retirin' modesty and dignity of the fair sect, and how shameful and revoltin' it would be to see wimmin throwin' 'em away and boldly and unblushin'ly talkin' about law and justice.

Why, to hear Betsey Bobbet talk about wimmin's throwin' their modesty away, you would think if they ever went to the political pole they would have to take their dignity and modesty and throw 'em against the pole and go without any all the rest of their lives.

Now I don't believe in no such stuff as that. I think a woman can be bold and unwomanly in other things besides goin' with a thick veil over her face, and a brass-mounted parasol, once a year, and gently and quietly dropping a vote for a Christian President, or a religious and noble-minded pathmaster.

She thinks she talks dreadful polite and proper. She says "I was cameing," instead of "I was coming"; and "I have saw," instead of "I have seen"; and "papah" for paper, and "deah" for dear. I don't know much about grammer, but common sense goes a good ways. She writes the poetry for the *Jonesville Augur*, or "Augah," as she calls it. She used to write for the opposition paper, the *Jonesville Gimlet*, but the editor of the *Augur*, a longhaired chap, who moved into Jonesville a few months ago, lost his wife soon after he come there, and sense that she has turned Dimocrat, and writes for his paper stidy. They say that he is a dreadful big feelin' man, and I have heard--it came right straight to me--his cousin's wife's sister told it to the mother-in-law of one of my neighbors' brother's wife, that he didn't like Betsey's poetry at all, and all he printed it for was to plague the editor of the *Gimlet*, because she used to write for him. I myself wouldn't give a cent a bushel for all the poetry she can write. And it seems to me, that if I was Betsey, I wouldn't try to write so much. Howsumever, I don't know what turn I should take if I was Betsey Bobbet; that is a solemn subject, and one I don't love to think on.

I never shall forget the first piece of her poetry I ever see. Josiah Allen and I had both on us been married goin' on a year, and I had occasion to go to his trunk one day, where he kept a lot of old papers, and the first thing I laid my hand on was these verses. Josiah went with her a few times after his wife died, on Fourth of July or so, and two or three camp-meetin's and the poetry seemed to be wrote about the time *we* was married. It was directed over the top of it, "Owed to Josiah," just as if she were in debt to him. This was the way it read:

"OWED TO JOSIAH

"Josiah, I the tale have hurn,
 With rigid ear, and streaming eye,
 I saw from me that you did turn,
 I never knew the reason why.
     Oh, Josiah,
     It seemed as if I must expiah.

"Why did you--oh, why did you blow
 Upon my life of snowy sleet,
 The fiah of love to fiercest glow,
 Then turn a damphar on the heat?
     Oh, Josiah,
     It seemed as if I must expiah.

"I saw thee coming down the street,
 She by your side in bonnet bloo,
 The stuns that grated 'neath thy feet,
 Seemed crunching on my vitals, too.
     Oh, Josiah,
     It seemed as if I must expiah.

"I saw thee washing sheep last night,
  On the bridge I stood with marble brow.
  The waters raged, thou clasped it tight,
  I sighed, 'should both be drownded now'-
      I thought, Josiah,
      Oh, happy sheep to thus expiah."

I showed the poetry to Josiah that night after he came home, and told him I had read it. He looked awful ashamed to think I had seen it, and, says he, with a dreadful sheepish look: "The persecution I underwent from that female can never be told; she fairly hunted me down. I hadn't no rest for the soles of my feet. I thought one spell she would marry me in spite of all I could do, without givin' me the benefit of law or gospel." He see I looked stern, and he added, with a sick-lookin' smile, "I thought one spell, to use Betsey's language, 'I was a gonah.'"

I didn't smile. Oh, no, for the deep principle of my sect was reared up. I says to him in a tone cold enough to almost freeze his ears: "Josiah Allen, shet up; of all the cowardly things a man ever done, it is goin 'round braggin' about wimmin likin' 'em, and follern' 'em up. Enny man that'll do that is little enough to crawl through a knot-hole without rubbing his clothes." Says I: "I suppose you made her think the moon rose in your head and set in your heels. I daresay you acted foolish enough round her to sicken a snipe, and if you makes fun of her now to please me, I let you know you have got holt of the wrong individual.

"Now," says I, "go to bed"; and I added, in still more freezing accents, "for I want to mend your pantaloons." He gathered up his shoes and stockin's and started off to bed, and we hain't never passed a word on the subject sence. I believe when you disagree with your pardner, in freein' your *mind* in the first on't, and then not to be a-twittin' about it afterward. And as for bein' jealous, I should jest as soon think of bein' jealous of a meetin'-house as I should of Josiah. He is a well-princi-pled man. And I guess he wasn't fur out o' the way about Betsey Bobbet, though I wouldn't encourage him by lettin' him say a word on the subject, for I always make it a rule to stand up for my own sect; but when I hear her go on about the editor of the *Augur*, I can believe anything about Betsey Bobbet.

She came in here one day last week. It was about ten o'clock in the morning.

I had got my house slick as a pin, and my dinner under way (I was goin' to have a b'iled dinner, and a cherry puddin' b'iled with sweet sass to eat on it), and I sot down to finish sewin' up the breadth of my new rag carpet. I thought I would get it done while I hadn't so much to do, for it bein' the first of March I knew sugarin' would be comin' on, and then cleanin'-house time, and I wanted it to put down jest as soon as the stove was carried out in the summer kitchen. The fire was sparklin' away, and the painted floor a-shinin' and the dinner a-b'ilin', and I sot there sewin' jest as calm as a clock, not dreamin' of no trouble, when in came Betsey Bobbet.

I met her with outward calm, and asked her to set down and lay off her things. She sot down but she said she couldn't lay off her things. Says she: "I was comin' down past, and I thought I would call and let you see the last numbah of the *Augah*. There is a piece in it concernin' the tariff that stirs men's souls. I like it evah so much."

She handed me the paper folded, so I couldn't see nothin' but a piece of poetry by Betsey Bobbet. I see what she wanted of me, and so I dropped my breadths of carpetin' and took hold of it, and began to read it.

"Read it audible, if you please," says she. "Especially the precious remahks ovah it; it is such a feast for me to be a-sittin' and heah it rehearsed by a musical vorce."

Says I, "I s'pose I can rehearse it if it will do you any good," so I began as follows:

"It is seldom that we present the readers of the *Augur* (the best paper for the fireside in Jonesville or the world) with a poem like the following. It may be, by the assistance of the *Augur* (only twelve shillings a year in advance, wood and potatoes taken in exchange), the name of Betsey Bobbet will yet be carved on the lofty pinnacle of fame's towering pillow. We think, however, that she could study such writers as Sylvanus Cobb and Tupper with profit both to herself and to them.

"Editor of the Augur."

Here Betsey interrupted me. "The deah editah of the *Augah* has no need to advise me to read Tuppah, for he is indeed my most favorite authar. You have devorhed him, haven't you, Josiah's Allen wife?"

"Devoured who?" says I, in a tone pretty near as cold as a cold icicle.

"Mahten, Fahqueah, Tuppah, that sweet authar," says she.

"No, mom," says I shortly; "I hain't devoured Martin Farquhar Tupper, nor no other man. I hain't a cannibal."

"Oh! you understand me not; I meant, devorhed his sweet, tender lines."

"I hain't devoured his tenderlines, nor nothin' relatin' to him," and I made a motion to lay the paper down, but Betsey urged me to go on, and so I read:

"GUSHINGS OF A TENDAH SOUL

"Oh let who will,
Oh let who can,
Be tied onto
A horrid male man.

"Thus said I 'ere
My tendah heart was touched,
Thus said I 'ere
My tendah feelings gushed.

"But oh a change
Hath swept ore me,
As billows sweep
The 'deep blue sea.'

"A voice, a noble form
One day I saw;
An arrow flew,
My heart is nearly raw.

"His first pardner lies
Beneath the turf,
He is wandering now,
In sorrow's briny surf.

"Two twins, the little

Deah cherub creechahs
Now wipe the teahs
From off his classic feachahs.

"Oh sweet lot, worthy
Angel arisen,
To wipe teahs
From eyes like hisen.

"What think you of it?" says she, as I finished readin'.

I looked right at her 'most a minute with a majestic look. In spite of her false curls and her new white ivory teeth, she is a humbly critter. I looked at her silently while she sot and twisted her long yellow bunnet-strings, and then I spoke out. "Hain't the editor of the *Augur* a widower with a pair of twins?"

"Yes," says she with a happy look.

Then says I, "If the man hain't a fool, he'll think you are one."

"Oh!" says she, and she dropped her bunnet-strings and clasped her long bony hands together in her brown cotton gloves. "Oh, we ahdent soles of genious have feelin's you cold, practical natures know nuthing of, and if they did not gush out in poetry we should expiah. You may as well try to tie up the gushing catarack of Niagarah with a piece of welting-cord as to tie up the feelin's of an ahdent sole."

"Ardent sole!" says I coldly. "Which makes the most noise, Betsey Bobbet, a three-inch brook or a ten-footer? which is the tearer? which is the roarer? Deep waters run stillest. I have no faith in feelin's that stalk round in public in mournin' weeds. I have no faith in such mourners," says I.

"Oh, Josiah's wife, cold, practical female being, you know me not; we are sundered as fah apart as if you was sitting on the North Pole and I was sitting on the South Pole. Uncongenial being, you know me not."

"I may not know you, Betsey Bobbet, but I do know decency, and I know that no munny would tempt me to write such stuff as that poetry and send it to a widower with twins."

"Oh!" says she, "what appeals to the tendah feelin' heart of a single female woman more than to see a lonely man who has lost his relict? And pity never seems so much like pity as when it is given to the deah little children of widowehs. And," says she, "I think moah than as likely as not, this soaring sole of genious did not wed his affinity, but was united to a mere woman of clay."

"Mere woman of clay!" says I, fixin' my spektacles upon her in a most searchin' manner. "Where will you find a woman, Betsey Bobbet, that hain't more or less clay? And affinity, that is the meanest word I ever heard; no married woman has any right to hear it. I'll excuse you, bein' a female; but if a man had said it to me I'd holler to Josiah. There is a time for everything, and the time to hunt affinity is before you are married; married folks hain't no right to hunt it," says I sternly.

"We kindred soles soah above such petty feelin's--we soah far above them."

"I hain't much of a soarer," says I, "and I don't pretend to be; and to tell you the truth," says I, "I am glad I ain't."

"The editah of the *Augah*" says she, and she grasped the paper offen the stand, and folded it up, and presented it at me like a spear, "the editah of this paper is a kindred sole: he appreciates me, he undahstands me, and will not our names in the pages of this very papah go down to posterety togathah?"

"Then," says I, drove out of all patience with her, "I wish you was there now, both of you. I wish," says I, lookin' fixedly on her, "I wish you was both of you in posterity now."

Fitzhugh Ludlow
SELECTIONS FROM A BRACE OF BOYS

I am a bachelor uncle. That, as a mere fact, might happen to anybody; but I am a bachelor uncle by internal fitness. I am one essentially, just as I am an individual of the Caucasian division of the human race; and if, through untoward circumstances--which heaven forbid--I should lose my present position, I shouldn't be surprised if you saw me out in the *Herald* under "Situations Wanted--Males." Thanks to a marrying tendency in the rest of my family, I have now little need to advertise, all the business being thrown into my way which a single member of my profession can attend to.

I meander, like a desultory, placid river of an old bachelor as I am, through the flowery mead of several nurseries, but I am detained longest among the children of my sister Lu.

Lu married Mr. Lovegrove. He is a merchant, retired with a fortune amassed by the old-fashioned, slow processes of trade, and regards the mercantile life of the present day only as so much greed and gambling Christianly baptized.... Lu is my favorite sister; Lovegrove an unusually good article of brother-in-law; and I cannot say that any of my nieces and nephews interest me more than their two children, Daniel and Billy, who are more unlike than words can paint them. They are far apart in point of years; Daniel is twenty-two, Bill eleven. I was reminded of this fact the other day by Billy, as he stood between my legs, scowling at his book of sums.

"'A boy has eighty-five turnips and gives his sister thirty'--pretty present for a girl, isn't it?" said Billy, with an air of supreme contempt, "Could *you* stand such stuff--say?"

I put on my instructive face and answered:

"Well, my dear Billy, you know that arithmetic is necessary to you if you mean to be an industrious man and succeed in business. Suppose your parents were to lose all their property, what would become of them without a little son who could make money and keep accounts?"

"Oh," said Billy, with surprise, "hasn't father got enough stamps to see him through?"

"He has now, I hope; but people don't always keep them. Suppose they should go by some accident, when your father was too old to make any more stamps for himself?"

"You haven't thought of Brother Daniel--"

True; for nobody ever had in connection with the active employments of life.

"No, Billy," I replied, "I forgot him; but then, you know, Daniel is more of a student than a business man, and--"

"Oh, Uncle Teddy! you don't think I mean he'd support them? I meant I'd have to take care of father and mother and him, too, when they'd all got to be old people together. Just think! I'm eleven, and he's twenty-two; so he is just twice as old as I am. How old are you?"

"Forty, Billy, last August."

"Well, you aren't so awful old, and when I get to be as old as you, Daniel will be eighty. Seth Kendall's grandfather isn't more than that, and he has to be fed with a spoon, and a nurse puts him to bed, and wheels him round in a chair like a baby. That takes the stamps, I bet! Well, I tell you how I'll keep my accounts: I'll have a stick like Robinson Crusoe, and every time I make a toadskin I'll gouge a piece out of one side of the stick, and every time I spend one I'll gouge a piece out of the other."

"Spend a *what?*" said the gentle and astonished voice of my sister Lu, who, unperceived, had slipped into the room.

"A toadskin, ma," replied Billy, shutting up Oolburn with a farewell glance of contempt.

"Dear, dear! Where does the boy learn such horrid words?"

"Why, ma, don't you know what a toadskin is? Here's one," said Billy, drawing a dingy five-cent stamp from his pocket. "And don't I wish I had lots of 'em!"

"Oh!" sighed his mother, "to think I should have a child so addicted to slang! How I wish he were like Daniel!"

"Well, mother," replied Billy, "if you wanted two boys just alike you'd oughter had twins. There ain't any use of my trying to be like Daniel now, when he's got eleven years the start. Whoop! There's a dog fight; hear 'em! It's Joe Casey's dog--I know his bark!"

With these words my nephew snatched his Glengarry bonnet from the table and bolted downstairs to see the fun.

"What will become of him?" said Lu hopelessly; "he has no taste for anything but rough play; and then such language as he uses! Why *isn't* he like Daniel?" "I suppose because his maker never repeats himself. Even twins often possess strongly marked individualities. Don't you think it would be a good plan to learn Billy better before you try to teach him? If you do, you'll make something as good of him as Daniel; though it will be rather different from that model."

"Remember, Ned, that you never did like Daniel as well as you do Billy. But we all know the proverb about old maid's daughters and old bachelor's sons. I wish you had Billy for a month--then you'd see."

"I'm not sure that I'd do any better than you. I might err as much in other directions. But I'd try to start right by acknowledging that he was a new problem, not to be worked without finding out the value of X in his particular instance. The formula which solves one boy will no more solve the next one than the rule of three will solve a question in calculus--or, to rise into your sphere, than the receipt for one-two-three-fourcake will conduct you to a successful issue through plum pudding."

I excel in metaphysical discussion, and was about giving further elaboration to my favorite idea, when the door burst open. Master Billy came tumbling in with a torn jacket, a bloody nose, the traces of a few tears in his eyes, and the mangiest of cur dogs in his hands.

"Oh my! my!! my!!!" exclaimed his mother.

"Don't you get scared, ma!" cried Billy, smiling a stern smile of triumph; "I smashed the nose off him! He won't sass me again for nothing *this* while. Uncle Teddy, d'ye know it wasn't a dog fight after all? There was that nasty, good-for-nothing Joe Casey, 'n Patsy Grogan, and a lot of bad boys from Mackerelville; and they'd caught this poor little ki-oodle and tied a tin pot to his tail, and were trying to set Joe's dog on him, though he's ten times littler."

"You naughty, naughty boy! How did you suppose your mother'd feel to see you playing with those ragamuffins?"

"Yes, I *played* 'em! I polished 'em--that's the play I did! Says I, 'Put down that poor little pup; ain't you ashamed of yourself, Patsy Grogan? 'I guess you don't know who I am,' says he. That's the way they always say, Uncle Teddy, to make a fellow think they're some awful great fighters. So says I again, 'Well, you put down that dog, or I'll show you who I am'; and when he held on, I let him have it. Then he dropped the pup, and as I stooped to pick it up he gave me one on the bugle."

"Bugle! Oh! Ooh! Ooh!"

"The rest pitched in to help him; but I grabbed the pup, and while I was trying to give as good as I got--only a fellow can't do it well with only one hand, Uncle Teddy--up came a policeman, and the whole crowd ran away. So I got the dog safe, and here he is!"

With that Billy set down his "ki-oodle," bid farewell to every fear, and wiped his bleeding nose. The unhappy beast slunk back between the legs of his preserver and followed him out of the room, as Lu, with an expression of maternal despair, bore him away for the correction of his dilapidated raiment and depraved associations. I felt such sincere pride in this young Mazzini of the dog nation that I was vexed at Lu for bestowing on him reproof instead of congratulation; but she was not the only conservative who fails to see a good cause and a heroic heart under a bloody nose and torn jacket. I resolved that if Billy was punished he should have his recompense before long in an extra holiday at Barnum's or the Hippotheatron.

You already have some idea of my other nephew, if you have noticed that none of us, not even that habitual disrespecter of dignities, Billy, ever called him Dan. It would have seemed as incongruous as to call Billy William. He was one of those youths who never gave their parents a moment's uneasiness; who never had to have their wills broken, and never forgot to put on their rubbers or take an umbrella. In boyhood he was intended for a missionary. Had it been possible for him to go to Greenland's icy mountains without catching cold, or India's coral strand without getting bilious, his parents would have carried out their pleasing dream of contributing him to the world's evangelization. Lu and Mr. Lovegrove had no doubt that he would have been greatly blessed if he could have stood it....

Both she and his father always encouraged old manners in him. I think they took such pride in raising a peculiarly pale boy as a gardener does in getting a nice blanch on his celery, and so long as he was not absolutely sick, the graver he was the better. He was a sensitive plant, a violet by a mossy stone, and all that sort of thing....

At the time I introduce Billy, both Lu and her husband were much changed. They had gained a great deal in width of view and liberality of judgment. They read Dickens and Thackeray with avidity; went now and then to the opera; proposed to let Billy take a quarter at Dodworth's; had statues in their parlor without any thought of shame at their lack of petticoats, and did multitudes of things which, in their early married life, they would have considered shocking. . . . They would greatly have liked to see Daniel shine in society. Of his erudition they were proud even to worship. The young man never had any business, and his father never seemed to think of giving him any, knowing, as Billy would say, that he had stamps enough to "see him through." If Daniel liked, his father would have endowed a professorship in some college and given him the chair; but that would have taken him away from his own room and the family physician.

Daniel knew how much his parents wished him to make a figure in the world, and only blamed himself for his failure, magnanimously forgetting that they had crushed out the faculties which enable a man to mint the small change of every-day society in the exclusive cultivation of such as fit him for smelting its ponderous ingots. With that merciful blindness which alone prevents all our lives from becoming a horror of nerveless self-reproach, his parents were equally unaware of their share in the harm done him when they ascribed to a delicate organization the fact that, at an age when love runs riot in all healthy blood, he could not see a Balmoral without his cheeks rivaling the most vivid stripe in it. They flattered themselves that he would outgrow his bashfulness; but Daniel had no such hope, and frequently confided in me that he thought he should never marry at all.

About two hours after Billy's disappearance under his mother's convoy, the defender of the oppressed returned to my room bearing the dog under his arm. His cheeks shone with washing like a pair of waxy Spitzenbergs, and other indignities had been offered him to the extent of the brush and comb. He also had a whole jacket on....

Billy and I also obtained permission to go out together and be gone the entire afternoon. We put Crab on a comfortable bed of rags in an old shoebox, and then strolled hand-in-hand across that most delightful of New York breathing places-- Stuyvesant Square.

"Uncle Teddy," exclaimed Billy with ardor, "I wish I could do something to show you how much I think of you for being so good to me. I don't know how. Would it make you happy if I was to learn a hymn for you--a smashing big hymn- -six verses, long metre, and no grumbling?"

"No, Billy, you make me happy enough just by being a good boy."

"Oh, Uncle Teddy!" replied Billy decidedly. "I'm afraid I can't do it. I've tried so often, and always make such a mess of it." ...

We now got into a Broadway stage going down, and being unable, on account of the noise, to converse further upon those spiritual conflicts of Billy's which so much interested me, amused ourselves with looking out until just as we reached the Astor House, when he asked me where we were going.

"Where do you guess?" said I.

He cast a glance through the front window and his face became irradiated. Oh, there's nothing like the simple, cheap luxury of pleasing a child to create sunshine enough for the chasing away of the blues of adult devils!

"We're going to Barnum's!" said Billy, involuntarily clapping his hands.

So we were; and, much as stuck-up people pretend to look down on the place, I frequently am. Not only so, but I always see that class largely represented there when I do go. To be sure, they always make believe that they only come to amuse the children, or because they've country cousins visiting them, but never fail to refer to the vulgar set one finds there, and the fact of the animals smelling like any-thing but Jockey Club; yet I notice that after they've been in the hall three minutes they're as much interested as any of the people they come to pooh-pooh, and only put on the high-bred air when they fancy some of their own class are looking at them. I boldly acknowledge that I go because I like it. I am especially happy, to be sure, if I have a child along to go into ecstasies, and give me a chance, by asking questions, for the exhibition of that fund of information which is said to be one of my chief charms in the social circle, and on several occasions has led that portion of the public immediately about the Happy Family into the erroneous impression that I was Mr. Barnum glibly explaining his five hundred thousand curiosities.

On the present occasion we found several visitors of the better class in the room devoted to the aquarium. Among these was a young lady, apparently about nineteen, in a tight-fitting basque of black velvet, which showed her elegant figure to fine advantage, a skirt of garnet silk, looped up over a pretty Balmoral, and the daintiest imaginable pair of kid walking-boots. Her height was a trifle over the medium; her eyes, a soft, expressive brown, shaded by masses of hair which exactly matched their color, and, at that rat-and-miceless day, fell in such graceful abandon as to show at once that nature was the only maid who crimped their waves into them. Her complexion was rosy with health and sympathetic enjoyment; her mouth was faultless, her nose sensitive, her manners full of refinement, and her voice as musical as a wood-robin's when she spoke to the little boy of six at her side, to whom she was revealing the palace of the great show-king. Billy and I were flattening our noses against the abode of the balloon fish and determining whether he looked most like a horse- chestnut burr or a ripe cucumber, when his eyes and my own simultaneously fell on the child and lady. In a moment, to Billy the balloon fish was as though he had not been.

"That's a pretty little boy," said I. And then I asked Billy one of those senseless routine questions which must make children look at us, regarding the scope of our intellects very much as we look at Bushmen.

"How would you like to play with him?"

"Him!" replied Billy scornfully, "that's his first pair of boots; see him pull up his little breeches to show the red tops to 'em! But, crackey! isn't *she* a smasher?"

After that we visited the wax figures and the sleepy snakes, the learned seal, and the glass-blowers. Whenever we passed from one room into another Billy could be caught looking anxiously to see if the pretty girl and child were coming too.

Time fails me to describe how Billy was lost in astonishment at the Lightning Calculator--wanted me to beg the secret of that prodigy for him to do his sums by--finally thought he had discovered it, and resolved to keep his arm whirling all the time he studied his arithmetic lesson the next morning. Equally inadequate is it to relate in full how he became so confused among the wax-works that he pinched the solemnest showman's legs to see if he was real, and perplexed the beautiful Circassian to the verge of idiocy by telling her he had read in his geography all about the way they sold girls like her.

We had reached the stairs to that subterranean chamber in which the Behemoth of Holy Writ was wallowing about without a thought of the dignity which one expects from a canonical character. Billy had always languished upon his memories of this diverting beast, and I stood ready to see him plunge headlong the moment that he read the signboard at the head of the stairs. When he paused and hesitated there, not seeming at all anxious to go down till he saw the pretty girl and the child following after--a sudden intuition flashed across me. Could it be possible that Billy was caught in that vortex which whirled me down at ten years--a little boy's first love?

We were lingering about the elliptical basin, and catching occasional glimpses between bubbles of a vivified hair trunk of monstrous compass, whose knobby lid opened at one end and showed a red morocco lining, when the pretty girl, in leaning over to point out the rising monster, dropped into the water one of her little gloves, and the swash made by the hippopotamus drifted it close under Billy's hand. Either in play or as a mere coincidence the animal followed it. The other children about the tank screamed and started back as he bumped his nose against the side; but Billy manfully bent down and grabbed the glove not an inch from one of his big tusks, then marched around the tank and presented it to the lady with a chivalry of manner in one of his years quite surprising.

"That's a real nice boy--you said so, didn't you, Lottie?--and I wish he'd come and play with me," said the little fellow by the young lady's side, as Billy turned away, gracefully thanked, to come back to me with his cheeks roseate with blushes.

As he heard this Billy idled along the edge of the tank for a moment, then faced about and said:

"P'raps I will some day. Where do you live?"

"I live on East Seventeenth Street with papa--and Lottie stays there, too, now--she's my cousin. Where d'you live?"

"Oh! I live close by--right on that big green square, where I guess the nurse takes you once in awhile," said Billy patronizingly. Then, looking up pluckily at the young lady, he added, "I never saw you out there."

"No; Jimmy's papa has only been in his new house a little while, and I've just come to visit him."

"Say, will you come and play with me some time?" chimed in the inextinguishable Jimmy. "I've got a cooking-stove--for real fire--and blocks, and a ball with a string."

Billy, who belonged to a club for the practise of the great American game, and was what A. Ward would call the most superior battist among the I. G. B. B. 0., or "Infant Giants," smiled from an altitude upon Jimmy, but promised to go and play with him the next Saturday afternoon.

Late that evening, after we had got home and dined, as I sat in my room over "Pickwick" with a sedative cigar, a gentle knock at the door told of Daniel. I called "Come in!" and, entering with a slow, dejected air, he sat down by my fire. For ten minutes he remained silent, though occasionally looking up as if about to speak, then dropping his head again, to ponder on the coals. Finally I laid down Dickens and spoke myself:

"You don't seem well to-night, Daniel?"

"I don't feel very well, uncle."

"What's the matter, my boy?"

"Oh-ah, I don't know. That is, I wish I knew how to tell you."

I studied him for a few minutes with kindly curiosity, then answered:

"Perhaps I can save you the trouble by cross-examining it out of you. Let's try the method of elimination. I know that you're not harassed by any economical considerations, for you've all the money you want; and I know that ambition doesn't trouble you, for your tastes are scholarly. This narrows down the investigation of your symptoms-- listlessness, general dejection, and all--to three causes--dyspepsia, religious conflicts, love. Now, is your digestion awry?"

"No, sir; good as usual. I'm not melancholy on religion, and--"

"You don't tell me you're in love?"

"Well,--yes--I suppose that's about it, Uncle Teddy."

I took a long breath to recover from my astonishment at this unimaginable revelation, then said: "Is your feeling returned?"

"I really don't know, uncle; I don't believe it is. I don't see how it can be. I never did anything to make her love me. What is there in me to love? I've borne nothing for her--that is, nothing that could do her any good--though I've endured on her account, I may say, anguish. So, look at it any way you please, I neither am, do nor suffer anything that can get a woman's love."

"Oh, you man of learning! Even in love you tote your grammar along with you, and arrange a divine passion under the active, passive and neuter!"

Daniel smiled faintly.

"You've no idea, Uncle Teddy, that you are twitting on facts; but you hit the truth there; indeed, you do. If she were a Greek or Latin woman I could talk Anacreon or Horace to her. If women only understood the philosophy of the flowers as well as they do the poetry--"

"Thank God they don't, Daniel!" sighed I devoutly.

"Never mind--in that case I could entrance her for hours, talking about the grounds of differences between Linnaeus and Jussieu. Women like the star business, they say--and I could tell her where all the constellations are; but sure as I tried to get off any sentiment about them, I'd break down and make myself ridiculous. But what earthly chance would the greatest philosopher that ever lived have with the woman he loved if he depended for her favor on his ability to analyze her bouquet or tell her when she might look out for the next occultation of Orion? I can't talk bread-and-butter talk. I can't do anything that makes a man even tolerable to a woman!"

"I hope you don't mean that nothing but bread-and-butter talk is tolerable to a woman!"

"No; but it's necessary to some extent--at any rate, the ability is-- in order to succeed in society; and it's in society men first meet and strike women. And, oh, Uncle Teddy! I'm such a fish out of water in society!--such a dreadful floundering fish! When I see her dancing gracefully as a swan swims, and feel that fellows like little Jack Mankyn, who 'don't know twelve times,' can dance to her perfect admiration; when I see that she likes ease of manners--and all sorts of men without an idea in their heads have that--while I turn all colors when I speak to her, and am clumsy, and abrupt, and abstracted, and bad at repartee--Uncle Teddy! sometimes (though it seems so ungrateful to father and mother, who have spent such pains for me)--sometimes, do you know, it seems to me as if I'd exchange all I've ever learned for the power to make a good appearance before her!"

"Daniel, my boy, it's too much a matter of reflection with you! A woman is not to be taken by laying plans. If you love the lady (whose name I don't ask you, because

I know you'll tell me as soon as you think best), you must seek her companionship until you're well enough acquainted with her to have her regard you as something different from the men whom she meets merely in society, and judge your qualities by another standard than that she applies to them. If she's a sensible girl (and God forbid you should marry her otherwise), she knows that people can't always be dancing, or holding fans, or running after orange-ice. If she's a girl capable of appreciating your best points (and woe to you if you marry a girl who can't!), she'll find them out upon closer intimacy, and, once found, they'll a hundred times outweigh all brilliant advantages kept in the show-case of fellows who have nothing on the shelves. When this comes about, you will pop the question unconsciously, and, to adapt Milton, she'll drop into your lap, 'gathered--not harshly plucked.'"

"I know that's sensible, Uncle Teddy, and I'll try. Let me tell you the sacredest of secrets--regularly every day of my life I send her a little poem fastened round the prettiest bouquet I can get at Hanft's."

"Does she know who sends them?"

"She can't have any idea. The German boy that takes them knows not a word of English except her name and address. You'll forgive me, uncle, for not mentioning her name yet? You see, she may despise or hate me some day when she knows who it is that has paid her these attentions; and then I'd like to be able to feel that at least I've never hurt her by any absurd connection with myself."

"Forgive you? Nonsense! The feeling does your heart infinite credit, though a little counsel with your head will show you that your only absurdity is self-depreciation."

Daniel bid me good-night. As I put out my cigar and went to bed my mind reverted to the dauntless little Hotspur who had spent the afternoon with me and reversed his mother's wish, thinking:

"Oh, if Daniel were more like Billy!"

It was always Billy's habit to come and sit with me while I smoked my after-breakfast cigar, but the next morning did not see him enter my room until St. George's hands pointed to a quarter of nine.

"Well, Billy Boy Blue, come blow your horn; what haystack have you been under till this time of day? We shan't have a minute to look over our spelling together, and I know a boy who's going in for promotion next week. Have you had your breakfast and taken care of Orab?"

"Yes, sir; but I didn't feel like getting up this morning."

"Are you sick?"

"No-o-o--it isn't that; but you'll laugh at me if I tell you."

"Indeed I won't, Billy!"

"Well"--his voice dropped to a whisper, and he stole close to my side--"I had such a nice dream about *her* just the last thing before the bell rang; and when I woke up I felt so queer--so kinder good and kinder bad--and I wanted to see her so much that, if I hadn't been a big boy, I believe I should have blubbered. I tried ever so much to go to sleep and see her again; but the more I tried the more I couldn't. After all, I had to get up without it, though I didn't want any breakfast, and only ate two buckwheat cakes, when I always eat six, you know, Uncle Teddy. Can you keep a secret?"

"Yes, dear, so you couldn't get it out of me if you were to shake me upside-down like a savings bank."

"Oh, ain't you mean! That was when I was small I did that. I'll tell you the secret, though--that girl and I are going to get married. I mean to ask her the first chance I get. Oh, isn't she a smasher!"

"My dear Billy, won't you wait a little while to see if you always like her as well as you do now? Then, too, you'll be older."

"I'm old enough, Uncle Teddy, and I love her dearly! I'm as old as the kings of France used to be when they got married--I read it in Abbott's histories. But there's the clock striking nine! I must run or I shall get a tardy mark, and, perhaps, she'll want to see my certificate sometimes."

So saying, he kissed me on the cheek and set off for school as fast as his legs could carry him. Oh, Love, omnivorous Love, that sparest neither the dotard leaning on his staff nor the boy with pantaloons buttoning on his jacket--omnipotent Love, that, after parents and teachers have failed, in one instant can make Billy try to become a good boy!

With both of my nephews hopelessly enamored and myself the confidant of both, I had my hands full. Daniel was generally dejected and distrustful; Billy buoyant and jolly. Daniel found it impossible to overcome his bashfulness; was spontaneous only in sonnets, brilliant only in bouquets. Billy was always coming to me with pleasant news, told in his slangy New York boy vernacular. One day he would exclaim: "Oh, I'm getting on prime! I got such a smile off her this morning as I went by the window!" Another day he wanted counsel how to get a valentine to her--because it was too big to shove in a lamp-post, and she might catch him if he left it on the steps, rang the bell and ran away. Daniel wrote his own valentine; but, despite its originality, that document gave him no such comfort as Billy got from his twenty- five cents' worth of embossed paper, pink cupids and doggerel. Finally Billy announced to me that he had been to play with Jimmy and got introduced to his girl.

Shortly after this Lu gave what they call "a little company"--not a party, but a reunion of forty or fifty people with whom the family were well acquainted, several of them living in our immediate neighborhood. There was a goodly proportion of young folk, and there was to be dancing; but the music was limited to a single piano played by the German exile usual on such occasions, and the refreshments did not rise to the splendor of a costly supper. This kind of compromise with fashionable gaiety was wisely deemed by Lu the best method of introducing Daniel to the ***beau monde***--a push given the timid eaglet by the maternal bird, with a soft tree-top between him and the vast expanse of society. How simple was the entertainment may be inferred from the fact that Lu felt somewhat discomposed when she got a note from one of her guests asking leave to bring along her niece, who was making her a few weeks' visit. As a matter of course, however, she returned answer to bring the young lady, and welcome.

Daniel's dressing-room having been given up to the gentlemen, I invited him to make his toilet in mine, and, indeed, wanting him to create a favorable impression, became his valet ***pro tem***, tying his cravat and teasing the divinity student look out of his side hair. My little dandy Billy came in for another share of attention, and when I managed to button his jacket for him so that it showed his shirt-studs "like a man's," Count d'Orsey could not have felt a more pleasing sense of his sufficiency for all the demands of the gay world.

When we reached the parlor we found Pa and and Ma Lovegrove already receiving. About a score of guests had arrived. Most of them were old married couples, which, after paying their ***devoirs***, fell in two like unriveted scissors--the gentlemen finding a new pivot in pa and the ladies in ma, where they mildly opened and shut upon such questions as severally concerned them, such as "the way gold closed" and "how the children were."

Besides the old married people, there were several old young men of distinctly hopeless and unmarried aspect who, having nothing in common with the other class, nor sufficient energy of character to band themselves for mutual protection, hovered dejectedly about the arch pillars or appeared to be considering whether, on the whole, it would not be feasible and best to sit down on the center table. These subsisted upon such crumbs of comfort as Lu could get an occasional chance to throw them by rapid sorties of conversation--became galvanically active the moment they were punched up and fell flat the moment the punching was remitted. I did all I could for them, but, having Daniel in tow, dared not sail too near the edge of the Doldrums, lest he should drop into sympathetic stagnation and be taken preternaturally bashful, with his sails all aback, just as I wanted to carry him gallantly into action with some clipper-built cruiser of a nice young lady. Finally, Lu bethought herself of that last plank of drowning conversationalists, the photograph album. All the dejected young men made for it at once, some reaching it just as they were about to sink for the last time, but all getting a grip on it somehow, and staying there in company with other people's babies whom they didn't know, and celebrities whom they knew to death, until, one by one, they either stranded upon a motherly dowager by the Fireplace Shoals, or were rescued from the Soda Reef by some gallant wrecker of a strong-minded young lady, with a view to taking salvage out of them in the German.

Besides these were already arrived a dozen nice little boys and girls, who had been invited to make it pleasant for Billy. I had to remind him of the fact that they were his guests, for, in comparison with the queen of his affections, they were in danger of being despised by him as small fry.

The younger ladies and gentlemen--those who had fascinations to disport or were in the habit of disporting what they considered such, were probably still at home consulting the looking-glass until that oracle should announce the auspicious moment for their setting forth.

Daniel was in conversation with a perfect godsend of a girl, who understood Latin and had begun Greek. Billy was taking a moment's vacation from his boys and girls, busy with "Old Maid" in the extension room, and whispering with his hand in mine, "Oh, don't I wish *she* were here!" when a fresh invoice of ladies, just unpacked from the dressing-room in all the airy elegance of evening costume, floated through the door. I heard Lu say:

"Ah, Mrs. Rumbullion! Happy to see your niece, too. How d'ye do, Miss Pilgrim?"

At this last word Billy jumped as if he had been shot, and the bevy of ladies opening about sister Lu disclosed the charming face and figure of the pretty girl we had met at Barnum's.

Billy's countenance rapidly changed from astonishment to joy.

"Isn't that splendid, Uncle Teddy? Just as I was wishing it! It's just like the fairy books!" and, rushing up to the party of newcomers, "My dear Lottie!" cried he, "if I'd only known you were coming I'd have gone after you!"

As he caught her by the hand I was pleased to see her soft eyes brighten with gratification at his enthusiasm, but my sister Lu looked on naturally with astonishment in every feature.

"Why, Billy!" said she, "you ought not to call a strange young lady 'Lottie!' Miss Pilgrim, you must excuse my wild boy."

"And you must excuse my mother, Lottie," said Billy, affectionately patting Miss Pilgrim's rose kid, "for calling you a strange young lady. You are not strange at all--you're just as nice a girl as there is."

"There are no excuses necessary," said Miss Pilgrim, with a bewitching little laugh. "Billy and I know each other intimately well, Mrs. Lovegrove; and I confess that when I heard the lady aunt had been invited to visit was his mother, I felt all the more willing to infringe etiquette this evening by coming where I had no previous introduction."

"Don't you care!" said Billy encouragingly--"I'll introduce you to every one of our family; I know 'em, if you don't."

At this moment I came up as Billy's reinforcement, and fearing lest in his enthusiasm he might forget the canon of society which introduces a gentleman to a lady, not the lady to him, I ventured to suggest it delicately by saying:

"Billy, will you grant me the favor of a presentation to Miss Pilgrim?"

"In a minute, Uncle Teddy," answered Billy, considerably lowering his voice. "The older people first;" and after this reproof I was left to wait in the cold until he had gone through the ceremony of introducing to the young lady his father and his mother.

Billy, who had now assumed entire guardianship of Miss Pilgrim, with an air of great dignity intrusted her to my care and left us promenading while he went in search of Daniel. I myself looked in vain for that youth, whom I had not seen since the entrance of the last comers. Miss Pilgrim and I found a congenial common ground in Billy, whom she spoke of as one of the most delightfully original boys she had ever met--in fact, altogether the most fascinating young gentleman she had seen in New York society. You may be sure it wasn't Billy's left ear which burned when I made my responses.

In five minutes he reappeared to announce, in a tone of disappointment, that he could find Daniel nowhere. He could see a light through his keyhole, but the door was locked, and he could get no admittance. Just then Lu came up to present a certain--no, an uncertain--young man of the fleet stranded on parlor furniture earlier in the evening. To Lu's great astonishment Miss Pilgrim asked Billy's permission to leave. It was granted with all the courtesy of a *preux chevalier*, on the condition readily assented to by the lady that she should dance one lancers with him during the evening.

"Dear me!" exclaimed Lu, after Billy had gone back like a superior being to assist at the childish amusement of his contemporaries, "would anybody ever suppose that was our Billy?"

"I should, my dear sister," said I, with proud satisfaction; "but you remember I always was just to Billy."

Left free, I went myself to hunt up Daniel, I found his door locked and a light shining through the keyhole, as Billy had stated. I made no attempt to enter by knocking, but, going to my room and opening the window next his, leaned out as far as I could, shoved up his sash with my cane, and pushed aside his curtain. Such an unusual method of communication could not fail to bring him to the window with a rush. When he saw me he trembled like a guilty thing, his countenance fell, and, no longer able to feign absence, he unlocked his door and let me enter by the normal mode.

"Why, Daniel Lovegrove, my nephew, what does this mean? Are you sick?"
"Uncle Edward, I am not sick--and this means that I am a fool. Even a little boy

like Billy puts me to shame. I feel humbled to the very dust. I wish I'd been a missionary and got massacred by savages. Oh, that I'd been permitted to wear damp stockings in childhood, or that my mother hadn't carried me through the measles! If it weren't wrong to take my life into my own hands, I'd open that window, and--and--sit in a draft this very evening! Oh, yes! I'm just that bitter! Oh, oh, oh!"

And he paced the floor with strides of frenzy.

"Well, my dear fellow, let's look at the matter calmly a minute. What brought on this sudden attack? You seemed doing well enough the first ten minutes after we came down. I was only out of your sight long enough to speak to the Rumbullion party, who had just come in, and when I turned around you were gone. Now you are in this fearful condition. What is there in the Rumbullions to start you off on such a bender of bashfulness as this which I here behold?"

"Rumbullion indeed!" said Daniel. "A hundred Rumbullions could not make me feel as I do. But *she* can shake me into a whirlwind with her little finger; and *she* came with the Rumbullions!"

"What! D'you--Miss Pilgrim?"

"Miss Pilgrim!"

I labored with Daniel for ten minutes, using every encouragement and argument I could think of, and finally threatened him that I would bring up the whole Rumbullion party, Miss Pilgrim included, telling them that he had invited them to look at his conchological cabinet, unless he instantly shook the ice out of his manner and accompanied me downstairs. The dreadful menace had the desired effect. He knew that I would not scruple to fulfil it; and at the same time that it made him surrender, it also provoked him with me to a degree which gave his eyes and cheeks as fine a glow as I could have wished for the purpose of a favorable impression. The stimulus of wrath was good for him, and there was little tremor in his knees when he descended the stairs. Well-a-day! So Daniel and Billy were rivals!

The latter gentleman met us at the foot of the staircase.

"Oh, there you are, Daniel!" he said cheerily. "I was just going to look after you and Uncle Teddy. We've wanted you for the dances. We've had the lancers twice, and three round dances; and I danced the second lancers with Lottie. Now we're going to play some games--to amuse the children, you know," he added loftily, with the adult gesture of pointing his thumb over his shoulder at the extension room.

"Lottie's going to play, too; so will you and Daniel, won't you, uncle? Oh, here comes Lottie now! This is my brother, Miss Pilgrim--let me introduce him to you. I'm sure you'll like him. There's nothing he don't know."

Miss Pilgrim had just come to the newel-post of the staircase and, when she looked into Daniel's face, blushed like the red, red rose, losing her self-possession perceptibly more than Daniel.

The courage of weak warriors and timid gallants mounts as the opposite party's falls, and Daniel made out to say in a firm tone that it was long since he had enjoyed the pleasure of meeting Miss Pilgrim.

"Not since Mrs. Cramcroud's last sociable, I think," replied Miss Pilgrim, her cheeks and eyes still playing the telltale.

"Oho! so you don't want any introduction!" exclaimed Master Billy. "I didn't know you knew each other, Lottie?"

"I have met Mr. Lovegrove in society. Shall we go and join the plays?"

"To be sure we shall!" cried Billy. "You needn't mind--all the grown people are going, too."

On entering the parlor we found it as he had said. The guests being almost all well acquainted with each other, at the solicitation of jolly little Miss Bloomingal, sister Lu had consented to make a pleasant Christmas kind of time of it, in which everybody was permitted to be young again and romp with the rompiest. We played blindman's buff till we were tired of that--Daniel, to Lu's delight, coming out splendidly as blindman, and evincing such "cheek" in the style he hunted down and caught the ladies as satisfied me that nothing but his eyesight stood in the way of his making an audacious figure in the world. Then a pretty little girl, Tilly Turtelle, who seemed quite a premature flirt, proposed "doorkeeper"--a suggestion accepted with great *eclat* by all the children, several grown people assenting.

To Billy--quite as much on account of his shining prominence in the executive faculties as of his character as host--was committed the duty of counting out the first person to be sent into the hall. There were so many of us that "Aina maina mona mike" would not go quite round; but, with that promptness of expedient which belongs to genius, Billy instantly added on, "Intery-mintery-cutery-corn," and the last word of the cabalistic formula fell upon me--Edward Balbus. I disappeared into the entry amidst peals of happy laughter from both old and young, calling, when the door opened again to ask me whom I wanted, for the pretty lisping flirt who had proposed the game. After giving me a coquettish little chirrup of a kiss and telling me my beard scratched, she bade me on my return, send out to her "Mithter Billy Lovegrove." I obeyed her; my youngest nephew retired; and after a couple of seconds, during which Tilly undoubtedly got what she proposed the game for, Billy being a great favorite with the little girls, she came back, pouting and blushing, to announce that he wanted Miss Pilgrim. That young lady showed no mock-modesty, but arose at once and laughingly went out to her youthful admirer, who, as I afterward learned, embraced her ardently and told her he loved her better than any girl in the world. As he turned to go back she told him that he might send to her one of her juvenile cousins, Reginald Rumbullion. Now, whether because on this youthful Rumbullion's account Billy had suffered the pangs of that most terrible passion, jealousy, or from his natural enjoyment of playing practical jokes destructive of all dignity in his elders, Billy marched into the room, and, having shut the door behind him, paralyzed the crowded parlor by an announcement that Mr. Daniel Lovegrove was wanted.

I was standing at his side and could feel him tremble--see him turn pale.

"Dear me!" he whispered in a choking voice, "can she mean me?"

"Of course she does," said I. "Who else? Do you hesitate? Surely you can't refuse such an invitation from a lady?"

"No, I suppose not," said he mechanically. And amidst much laughter from the disinterested while the faces of Mrs. Rumbullion and his mother were spectacles of crimson astonishment, he made his exit from the room. Never in my life did I so much long for that instrument described by Mr. Samuel Weller--a pair of patent double-million- magnifying microscopes of hextry power, to see through a deal door. Instead of this, I had to learn what happened only by report.

Lottie Pilgrim was standing under the hall burners with her elbow on the newel-post, looking more vividly charming than he had ever seen her before at Mrs. Cramcroud's sociable or elsewhere. When startled by the apparition of Mr. Daniel Lovegrove instead of the little Rum- bullion whom she was expecting, she had no time to exclaim or hide her mounting color, none at all to explain to her own mind the mistake that had occurred, before his arm was clasped around her waist, and his lips so closely pressed to hers, that through her soft thick hair she could feel the throbbing of his temples. As for Daniel, he seemed in a walking dream, from which he waked to see Miss Pilgrim looking into his eyes with utter though not incensed stupefaction--to stammer:

"Forgive me! Do forgive me! I thought you were in earnest."

"So I was," she said tremulously, as soon as she could catch her voice, "in sending for my cousin Reginald."

"Oh, dear, what shall I do! Believe me, I was told you wanted me. Let me go and explain it to mother--she'll tell the rest. I couldn't do it--I'd die of mortification. Oh, that wretched boy Billy!"

On the principle already mentioned, his agitation reassured her.

"Don't try to explain it now--it may get Billy a scolding. Are there any but intimate family friends here this evening?"

"No--I believe--no--I'm sure," replied Daniel, collecting his faculties.

"Then I don't mind what they think. Perhaps they'll suppose we've known each other long; but we'll arrange it by-and-by. They'll think the more of it the longer we stay out here--hear them laugh! I must run back now. I'll send you somebody."

A round of juvenile applause greeted her as she hurried into the parlor, and a number of grown people smiled quite musically. Her quick woman wit showed her how to retaliate and divide the embarrassment of the occasion. As she passed me she said in an undersone:

"Answer quick! Who's that fat lady on the sofa, that laughs so loud?"

"Mrs. Cromwell Crags," said I as quietly.

Miss Pilgrim made a satirically low courtsey and spoke in a modest but distinct voice:

"I really must be excused for asking. I'm a stranger, you know; but is there such a lady here as Mrs. Craggs--Mrs. **Cromwell** Craggs? For if so, the present door-keeper would like to see Mrs. Cromwell Craggs."

Then came the turn of the fat lady to be laughed at; but out she had to go and get kissed like the rest of us.

Before the close of the evening Billy was made as jealous as his parents and I was surprised to see Daniel in close conversation with Miss Pilgrim among the geraniums and fuchsias of the conservatory. "A regular flirtation!" said Billy somewhat indignantly. The conclusion they arrived at was, that after all no great harm had been done, and that the dear little fellow ought not to be peached on for his fun. If I had known at the time how easily they forgave him, I should have suspected that the offense Billy had led Daniel into committing was not unlikely to be repeated on the offender's own account; but so much as I could see showed me that the ice was broken.

--From "Little Brother, and Other Genre Pictures."

Robert Jones Burdette
RHEUMATISM MOVEMENT CURE

One day, not a great while ago, Mr. Middlerib read in his favorite paper a paragraph stating that the sting of a bee was a sure cure for rheumatism, and citing several remarkable instances in which people had been perfectly cured by this abrupt remedy. Mr. Middlerib thought of the rheumatic twinges that grappled his knees once in awhile and made his life a burden.

He read the article several times and pondered over it. He understood that the stinging must be done scientifically and thoroughly. The bee, as he understood the article, was to be griped by the ears and set down upon the rheumatic joint and held there until it stung itself stingless. He had some misgivings about the matter. He knew it would hurt. He hardly thought it could hurt any worse than the rheumatism, and it had been so many years since he was stung by a bee that he had almost forgotten what it felt like. He had, however, a general feeling that it would hurt some. But desperate diseases require desperate remedies, and Mr. Middlerib was willing to undergo any amount of suffering if it would cure his rheumatism.

He contracted with Master Middlerib for a limited supply of bees; humming and buzzing about in the summer air, Mr. Middlerib did not know how to get them. He felt, however, that he could safely depend upon the instincts and methods of boyhood. He knew that if there was any way in heaven whereby the shyest bee that ever lifted a two hundred pound man off the clover could be induced to enter a wide- mouthed glass bottle, his son knew that way.

For the small sum of one dime Master Middlerib agreed to procure several, to wit: six bees, sex and age not specified; but, as Mr. Middlerib was left in uncertainty as to the race, it was made obligatory upon the contractor to have three of them honey and three humble, or, in the generally accepted vernacular, bumblebees. Mr.

M. did not tell his son what he wanted those bees for, and the boy went off on his mission with his head so full of astonishment that it fairly whirled. Evening brings all home, and the last rays of the declining sun fell upon Master Middlerib with a short, wide-mouthed bottle comfortably populated with hot, ill-natured bees, and Mr. Middlerib and a dime. The dime and the bottle changed hands. Mr. Middlerib put the bottle in his coat pocket and went into the house eyeing everybody he met very suspiciously, as though he had made up his mind to sting to death the first person who said "bee" to him. He confided his guilty secret to none of his family. He hid his bees in his bedroom, and as he looked at them just before putting them away he half wished the experiment was safely over. He wished the imprisoned bees did not look so hot and cross. With exquisite care he submerged the bottle in a basin of water and let a few drops in on the heated inmates to cool them off.

At the tea table he had a great fright. Miss Middlerib, in the artless simplicity of her romantic nature, said:

"I smell bees. How the odor brings up---"

But her father glared at her and said, with superfluous harshness and execrable grammar: "Hush up! You don't smell nothing."

Whereupon Mrs. Middlerib asked him if he had eaten anything that disagreed with him, and Miss Middlerib said:

"Why, pa!" and Master Middlerib smiled as he wondered.

Bedtime at last, and the night was warm and sultry. Under various false pretenses, Mr. Middlerib strolled about the house until everybody else was in bed, and then he sought his room. He turned the lamp down until its feeble ray shone dimly as a death-light.

Mr. Middlerib disrobed slowly--very slowly. When at last he was ready to go lumbering into his peaceful couch, he heaved a profound sigh, so full of apprehension and grief that Mrs. Middlerib, who was awakened by it, said if it gave him so much pain to come to bed perhaps he had better sit up all night. Mr. Middlerib choked another sigh, but said nothing and crept into bed. After lying still a few moments he reached out and got his bottle of bees.

It was not an easy thing to do to pick one bee out of the bottle with his fingers and not get into trouble. The first bee Mr. Middlerib got was a little brown honeybee, that wouldn't weigh half an ounce if you picked him up by the ears, but if you lifted him by the hind leg would weigh as much as the last end of a bay mule. Mr. Middlerib could not repress a groan.

"What's the matter with you?" sleepily asked his wife.

It was very hard for Mr. Middlerib to say he only felt hot, but he did it. He didn't have to lie about it, either. He did feel very hot indeed--about eighty-six all over, and one hundred and ninety-seven on the end of his thumb. He reversed the bee and pressed the warlike terminus of it firmly against the rheumatic knee.

It didn't hurt so badly as he thought it would.

It didn't hurt at all.

Then Mr. Middlerib remembered that when the honey-bee stabs a human foe it generally leaves its harpoon in the wound, and the invalid knew that the only thing this bee had to sting with was doing its work at the end of his thumb.

He reached his arm out from under the sheets and dropped this disabled atom of rheumatism liniment on the carpet. Then, after a second of blank wonder, he began to feel round for the bottle, and wished he knew what he did with it.

In the meantime strange things had been going on. When he caught hold of the first bee, Mr. Middlerib, for reasons, drew it out in such haste that for a time he forgot all about the bottle and its remedial contents, and left it lying uncorked in the bed, between himself and his innocent wife. In the darkness there had been a quiet but general emigration from that bottle. The bees, their wings clogged with the water Mr. Middlerib had poured upon them to cool and tranquillize them, were crawling aimlessly over the sheet. While Mr. Middlerib was feeling around for it, his ears were suddenly thrilled and his heart frozen by a wild, piercing scream from his wife.

"Murder!" she screamed. "Murder! Oh Help me! Help! Help!"

Mr. Middlerib sat bolt upright in bed. His hair stood on end. The night was warm, but he turned to ice in a minute.

"Where in thunder," he said, with pallid lips, as he felt all over the bed in frenzied haste, "where in thunder are them infernal bees?"

And a large "bumble," with a sting as pitiless as the finger of scorn, just then climbed up the inside of Mr. Middlerib's nightshirt, until it got squarely between his shoulders, and then it felt for his marrow, and he said calmly:

"Here is one of them."

And Mrs. Middlerib felt ashamed of her feeble screams when Mr. Middlerib threw up both arms and, with a howl that made the windows rattle, roared:

"Take him off! Oh, land of Scott, somebody take him off!"

And when the little honey-bee began tickling the sole of Mrs. Middlerib's foot, she shrieked that the house was bewitched, and immediately went into spasms.

The household was aroused by this time. Miss Middlerib and Master Middlerib and the servants were pouring into the room, adding to the general confusion by howling at random and asking irrelevant questions, while they gazed at the figure of a man a little on in years arrayed in a long night-shirt, pawing fiercely at the unattainable spot in the middle of his back, while he danced an unnatural, weird, wicked-looking jig by the dim, religious light of the night-lamp. And while he danced and howled, and while they gazed and shouted, a navy-blue wasp, that Master Middlerib had put in the bottle for good measure and variety, and to keep the menagerie stirred up, had dried his legs and wings with a corner of the sheet, and after a preliminary circle or two around the bed to get up his motion and settle down to a working gait, he fired himself across the room, and to his dying day Mr. Middlerib will always believe that one of the servants mistook him for a burglar and shot him.

No one, not even Mr. Middlerib himself, could doubt that he was, at least for the time, most thoroughly cured of rheumatism. His own boy could not have carried himself more lightly or with greater agility. But the cure was not permanent, and Mr. Middlerib does not like to talk about it.--New York Weekly.

Oliver Wendell Holmes
AN APHORISM AND A LECTURE

One of the boys mentioned, the other evening, in the course of a very pleasant poem he read us, a little trick of the Commons table- boarders, which I, nourished at the parental board, had never heard of. Young fellows being always hungry----Allow me to stop dead short, in order to utter an aphorism which has been forming itself in one of the blank interior spaces of my intelligence, like a crystal in the cavity of a geode.

Aphorism by the Professor

In order to know whether a human being is young or old, offer it food of different kinds at short intervals. If young, it will eat anything at any hour of the day or night. If old, it observes stated periods, and you might as well attempt to regulate the time of high-water to suit a fishing-party as to change these periods.

The crucial experiment is this. Offer a bulky and boggy bun to the suspected individual just ten minutes before dinner. If this is eagerly accepted and devoured, the fact of youth is established. If the subject of the question starts back and expresses surprise and incredulity, as if you could not possibly be in earnest, the fact of maturity is no less clear.

--Excuse me--I return to my story of the Commons table. Young fellows being always hungry, and tea and dry toast being the meager fare of the evening meal, it was a trick of some of the boys to impale a slice of meat upon a fork at dinner time and stick the fork holding it beneath the table, so that they could get it at tea time. The dragons that guarded this table of the Hesperides found out the trick at last and kept a sharp lookout for missing forks--they knew where to find one if it was not in its place. Now the odd thing was that, after waiting so many years to hear of this college trick, I should hear it mentioned a ***second time*** within the same twenty-four hours by a college youth of the present generation. Strange, but true. And so it has happened to me and to every person, often and often, to be hit in rapid succession by these twinned facts or thoughts, as if they were linked like chain-shot.

I was going to leave the simple reader to wonder over this, taking it as an unexplained marvel. I think, however, I will turn over a furrow of subsoil in it. The explanation is, of course, that in a great many thoughts there must be a few coincidences, and these instantly arrest our attention. Now we shall probably never have the least idea of the enormous number of impressions which pass through our consciousness, until in some future life we see the photographic record of our thoughts and the stereoscopic picture of our actions. There go more pieces to make up a conscious life or a living body than you think for. Why, some of you were surprised when a friend of mine told you there were fifty-eight separate pieces in a fiddle. How many "swimming glands"--solid, organized, regularly formed, rounded disks, taking an active part in all your vital processes, part and parcel, each one of them, of your corporal being--do you suppose are whirled along like pebbles in a stream with the blood which warms your frame and colors your cheeks? A noted German physiologist spread out a minute drop of blood under the microscope, in narrow streaks, and counted the globules, and then made a calculation. The counting by the micrometer took him a *week*. You have, my full-grown friend, of these little couriers in crimson or scarlet livery, running on your vital errands day and night as long as you live, sixty-five billions five hundred and seventy thousand millions, errors excepted. Did I hear some gentleman say "Doubted"? I am the Professor; I sit in my chair with a petard under it that will blow me through the skylight of my lecture-room if I do not know what I am talking about and whom I am quoting.

Now, my dear friends, who are putting your hands to your foreheads and saying to yourselves that you feel a little confused, as if you had been waltzing until things began to whirl slightly round you, is it possible that you do not clearly apprehend the exact connection of all that I have been saying and its bearing on what is now to come? Listen, then. The number of these living elements in our body illustrates the incalculable multitude of our thoughts; the number of our thoughts accounts for those frequent coincidences spoken of; these coincidences in the world of thought illustrate those which we constantly observe in the world of outward events, of which the presence of the young girl now at our table, and proving to be the daughter of an old acquaintance some of us may remember, is the special example which led me through this labyrinth of reflections, and finally lands me at the commencement of this young girl's story, which, as I said, I have found the time and felt the interest to learn something of, and which I think I can tell without wronging the unconscious subject of my brief delineation.

A Short Lecture on Phrenology

Read to the Boarders at Our Breakfast Table

I shall begin, my friends, with the definition of a pseudoscience. A pseudoscience consists of a *nomenclature*, with a self-adjusting arrangement, by which all positive evidence, or such as favors its doctrines, is admitted, and all negative evidence, or such as tells against it, is excluded. It is invariably connected with some lucrative practical application. Its professors and practitioners are usually shrewd people; they are very serious with the public, but wink and laugh a good deal among themselves. The believing multitude consists of women of both sexes, feeble-minded inquirers, poetical optimists, people who always get cheated in buying horses, philanthropists who insist on hurrying up the millennium, and others of this class, with here and there a clergyman, less frequently a lawyer, very rarely a physician, and almost never a horse-jockey or a member of the detective police. I did not say that Phrenology was one of the pseudosciences.

A pseudoscience does not necessarily consist wholly of lies. It may contain many truths, and even valuable ones. The rottenest bank starts with a little specie. It puts out a thousand promises to pay on the strength of a single dollar, but the dollar is very commonly a good one. The practitioners of the pseudosciences know that common minds after they have been baited with a real fact or two, will jump at the merest rag of a lie, or even at the bare hook. When we have one fact found us, we are very apt to supply the next out of our own imagination. (How many persons can read Judges XV. 16 correctly the first time?) The pseudosciences take advantage of this. I did not say that it was so with Phrenology.

I have rarely met a sensible man who would not allow that there was *something* in Phrenology. A broad, high forehead, it is commonly agreed, promises intellect; one that is "villainous low," and has a huge hind-head back of it, is wont to mark an animal nature. I have as rarely met an unbiased and sensible man who really believed in the bumps. It is observed, however, that persons with what the phrenologists call "good heads" are more prone than others toward plenary belief in the doctrine.

It is so hard to prove a negative that, if a man should assert that the moon was in truth a green cheese, formed by the coagulable substance of the Milky Way, and challenge me to prove the contrary, I might be puzzled. But if he offer to sell me a ton of this lunar cheese, I call on him to prove the truth of the caseous nature of our satellite before I purchase.

It is not necessary to prove the falsity of the phrenological statement. It is only necessary to show that its truth is not proved, and cannot be, by the common course of argument. The walls of the head are double, with a great air-chamber between them, over the smallest and most closely crowded "organs." Can you tell how much money there is in a safe, which also has thick double walls, by kneading its knobs with your fingers? So when a man fumbles about my forehead, and talks about the organs of **Individuality**, **Size**, etc., I trust him as much as I should if he felt of the outside of my strongbox and told me that there was a five-dollar or a ten-dollar bill under this or that particular rivet. Perhaps there is; **only he doesn't know anything about it**. But this is a point that I, the Professor, understand, my friends, or ought to, certainly, better than you do. The next argument you will all appreciate.

I proceed, therefore, to explain the self-adjusting mechanism of Phrenology, which is **very similar** to that of the pseudosciences. An example will show it most conveniently.

A-- is a notorious thief. Messrs. Bumpus and Crane examine him and find a good-sized organ of Acquisitiveness. Positive fact for Phrenology. Casts and drawings of A-- are multiplied, and the bump **does not lose** in the act of copying--I did not say it gained. --What do you look for so? (to the boarders).

Presently B-- turns up, a bigger thief than A--. But B-- has no bump at all over Acquisitiveness. Negative fact; goes against Phrenology. Not a bit of it. Don't you see how small Conscientiousness is? **That's** the reason B-- stole.

And then comes C--, ten times as much a thief as either A-- or B--; used to steal before he was weaned, and would pick one of his own pockets and put its contents in another, if he could find no other way of committing petty larceny. Unfortunately C-- has a **hollow**, instead of a bump, over Acquisitiveness. Ah! but just look and see what a bump of Alimentiveness! Did not O-- buy nuts and gingerbread, when a boy, with the money he stole? Of course you see why he is a thief, and how his example confirms our noble science.

At last comes along a case which is apparently a **settler**, for there is a little brain with vast and varied powers--a case like that of Byron, for instance. Then comes out the grand reserve--reason which covers everything and renders it simply impossible ever to corner a phrenologist. "It is not the size alone, but the **quality** of an organ, which determines its degree of power."

Oh! oh! I see. The argument may be briefly stated thus by the phrenologist: "Heads I win, tails you lose." Well, that's convenient. It must be confessed that Phrenology has a certain resemblance to the pseudosciences. I did not say it was a pseudoscience.

I have often met persons who have been altogether struck up and amazed at the accuracy with which some wandering Professor of Phrenology had read their characters written upon their skulls. Of course, the Professor acquires his information solely through his cranial inspections and manipulations. What are you laughing at? (to the boarders). But let us just **suppose**, for a moment, that a tolerably cunning fellow, who did not know or care anything about Phrenology, should open a shop and undertake to read off people's characters at fifty cents or a dollar apiece. Let us see how well he could get along without the "organs."

I will suppose myself to set up such a shop. I would invest one hundred dollars, more or less, in casts of brains, skulls, charts, and other matters that would make the most show for the money. That would do to begin with. I would then advertise myself as the celebrated Professor Brainey, or whatever name I might choose, and wait for my first customer--a middle-aged man. I look at him, ask him a question or two, so as to hear him talk. When I have got the hang of him, I ask him to sit down, and proceed to fumble his skull, dictating as follows:

SCALE FROM 1 TO 10

LIST OF FACULTIES FOR CUSTOMER--PRIVATE NOTES FOR MY PUPIL: **Each to be accompanied with a wink.**

Amativeness, 7   Most men love the conflicting sex, and all men
                        love to be told they do.

Alimentiveness, 8	Don't you see that he has burst off his lowest waistcoat button with feeding--hey?
Acquisitiveness, 8	Of course. A middle-aged Yankee.
Approbativeness, 7+	Hat well brushed. Hair ditto. Mark the effect of that plus sign.
Self-esteem, 6	His face shows that.
Benevolence, 9	That'll please him.

Conscientiousness, 8 1/2 That fraction looks first rate.

Mirthfulness, 7	Has laughed twice since he came in. That sounds well.

Ideality, 9

Form, Size, Weight,
Color, Locality,
Eventuality, etc.,   Average everything that can't be guessed.
etc. (4 to 6)

And so of other faculties

Of course, you know, that isn't the way the phrenologists do. They go only by the bumps. What do you keep laughing so for (to the boarders)? I only said that is the way I should practise "Phrenology" for a living.

Joshua S. Morris
THE HARP OF A THOUSAND STRINGS

A Hard-Shell Baptist Sermon

(This characteristic effusion first appeared in a New Orleans paper. The locality is supposed to be a village on the bank of the Mississippi River, whither the volunteer parson had brought his flatboat for the purpose of trade.)

I may say to you, my brethring, that I am not an edicated man, an' I am not one of them as believes that edication is necessary for a Gospel minister, for I believe the Lord edicates his preachers jest as he wants 'em to be edicated; an' although I say it that oughtn't to say it, yet in the State of Indianny, whar I live, thar's no man as gets bigger congregations nor what I gits.

Thar may be some here to-day, my brethring, as don't know what persuasion I am uv. Well, I must say to you, my brethring, that I'm a Hard-shell Baptist. Thar's some folks as don't like the Hard-shell Baptists, but I'd rather have a hard shell as no shell at all. You see me here to-day, my brethring, dressed up in fine clothes; you mout think I was proud, but I am not proud, my brethring, and although I've been a preacher of the Gospel for twenty years, an' although I'm capting of the flatboat that lies at your landing, I'm not proud, my brethring.

I am not gwine to tell edzactly whar my tex may be found; suffice to say, it's in the leds of the Bible, and you'll find it somewhar between the first chapter of the book of Generations and the last chapter of the book of Revolutions, and ef you'll go and search the Scriptures, you'll not only find my tex thar, but a great many other texes as will do you good to read, and my tex, when you shall find it, you shall find it to read thus:

"And he played on a harp uv a thousand strings, sperits uv jest men made per-feck."

My text, my brethring, leads me to speak of sperits. Now, thar's a great many kinds of sperits in the world--in the fuss place, thar's the sperits as some folks call ghosts, and thar's the sperits of turpentine, and thar's the sperits as some folks call liquor, an' I've got as good an artikel of them kind of sperits on my flatboat as ever was fotch down the Mississippi River; but thar's a great many other kinds of sperits, for the tex says, "He played on a harp uv a *t-h-o-u-s*-and strings, sperits uv jest men made perfeck."

But I tell you the kind uv sperits as is meant in the tex is FIRE. That's the kind uv sperits as is meant in the tex, my brethring. Now, thar's a great many kinds of fire in the world. In the fuss place, there's the common sort of fire you light your cigar or pipe with, and then thar's foxfire and camphire, fire before you're ready, and fire and fall back, and many other kinds uv fire, for the tex says, "He played *on* the harp uv a *thous*and strings, sperits of jest men made perfeck."

But I'll tell you the kind of fire as is meant in the tex, my brethring--it's HELL FIRE! an' that's the kind uv fire as a great many uv you'll come to, ef you don't do better nor what you have been doin'--for "He played on a harp uv a *thous*and strings, sperits uv jest men made perfeck."

Now, the different sorts of fire in the world may be likened unto the different persuasions of Christians in the world. In the first place, we have the Piscapalions, an' they are a high-sailin' and highfalutin' set, and they may be likened unto a tur-key buzzard that flies up into the air, and he goes up, and up, and up, till he looks no bigger than your finger nail, and the fust thing you know, he cums down, and down, and down, and is a-fillin' himself on the carkiss of a dead hoss by the side of the road, and "He played on a harp uv a *thous*and strings, sperits uv *jest* men made perfeck."

And then thar's the Methodis, and they may be likened unto the squirril run-nin' up into a tree, for the Methodis beleeves in gwine on from one degree of grace to another, and finally on to perfection, and the squirril goes up and up, and up and up, and he jumps from limb to limb, and branch to branch, and the fust thing you know he falls, and down he cums kerflumix, and that's like the Methodis, for they is allers fallen from grace, ah! and "He played on a harp uv a *thous*and strings, sperits of jest men made perfeck."

And then, my brethring, that's the Baptist, ah! and they have been likened unto a 'possum on a 'simmon tree, and thunders may roll and the earth may quake, but that 'possum clings thar still, ah! and you may shake one foot loose, an the other's thar, and you may shake all feet loose, and he laps his tail around the limb, and clings, and he clings furever, for "He played on the harp uv a *thous*and strings, sperits uv jest men made perfeck."

Seba Smith
MY FIRST VISIT TO PORTLAND

In the fall of the year 1829 I took it into my head I'd go to Portland. I had heard a good deal about Portland, what a fine place it was, and how the folks got rich there proper fast; and that fall there was a couple of new papers come up to our place from there, called the **Portland Courier** and **Family Reader**, and they told a good many queer kind of things about Portland, and one thing and another; and all at once it popped into my head, and I up and told father, and says:

"I'm going to Portland, whether or no; and I'll see what this world is made of yet."

Father stared a little at first and said he was afraid I would get lost; but when he see I was bent upon it, he give it up, and he stepped to his chist, and opened the till, and took out a dollar and gave it to me; and says he:

"Jack, this is all I can do for you; but go and lead an honest life, and I believe I shall hear good of you yet."

He turned and walked across the room, but I could see the tears start into his eyes. And mother sat down and had a hearty crying spell.

This made me feel rather bad for a minit or two, and I almost had a mind to give it up; and then again father's dream came into my mind, and I mustered up courage and declared I'd go. So I tackled up the old horse, and packed in a load of ax-handles and a few notions; and mother fried me some doughnuts and put 'em into a box, along with some cheese and sausages and ropped me up another shirt, for I told her I didn't know how long I should be gone. After I got rigged out, I went round and bid all the neighbors good-by and jumped in and drove off for Portland.

Aunt Sally had been married two or three years before and moved to Portland; and I inquired round till I found out where she lived and went there and put the old horse up, and ate some supper and went to bed.

And the next morning I got up and straightened right off to see the editor of the **Portland Courier**, for I knew by what I had seen in his paper that he was just the man to tell me which way to steer. And when I come to see him, I knew I was right; for soon as I told him my name and what I wanted, he took me by the hand as kind as if he had been a brother, and says he:

"Mister," says he, "I'll do anything I can to assist you. You have come to a good town. Portland is a healthy, thriving place, and any man with a proper degree of enterprise may do well here. But," says he, "stranger," and he looked mighty kind of knowing, says he, "if you want to make out to your mind, you must do as the steamboats do."

"Well," says I, "how do they do?" for I didn't know what a steamboat was any more than the man in the moon.

"Why," says he, "they go ahead. And you must drive about among the folks here just as tho' you were at home on the farm among the cattle. Don't be afraid of any of them, but figure away, and I dare say you'll get into good business in a very little while. But," says he, "there's one thing you must be careful of, and that is, not to get into the hands of those are folks that trades up round Hucklers' Row, for there's some sharpers up there, if they get hold of you, would twist your eye-teeth out in five minits."

Well, arter he had giv me all the good advice he could, I went back to Aunt Sally's agin and got some breakfast; and then I walked all over the town, to see what chance I could find to sell my ax-handles and things and to git into business.

After I had walked about three or four hours, I come along toward the upper end of the town, where I found there were stores and shops of all sorts and sizes. And I met a feller, and says I:

"What place is this?"

"Why, this," says he, "is Hucklers' Row."

"What," says I, "are these the stores where the traders in Hucklers' Row keep?"

And says he, "Yes."

Well, then, says I to myself, I have a pesky good mind to go in and have a try with one of these chaps and see if they can twist my eye- teeth out. If they can get the best end of the bargain out of me they can do what there ain't a man in our place can do; and I should just like to know what sort of stuff these ere Portland chaps are made of. So in I goes into the best-looking store among 'em. And I see some biscuit lying on the shelf, and says I:

"Mister, how much do you ax apiece for them ere biscuits?"

"A cent apiece," says he.

"Well," says I, "I shan't give you that, but if you've a mind to, I'll give you two cents for three of them, for I begin to feel a little as tho' I would like to take a bite."

"Well," says he, "I wouldn't sell 'em to anybody else so, but seeing it's you I don't care if you take 'em."

I knew he lied, for he never seen me before in his life. Well, he handed down the biscuits, and I took 'em, and walked round the store awhile, to see what else he had to sell. At last says I:

"Mister, have you got any good cider?"

Says he, "Yes, as good as ever you see."

"Well," says I, "what do you ax a glass for it?"

"Two cents," says he.

"Well," says I, "seems to me I feel more dry than I do hungry now. Ain't you a mind to take these ere biscuits again and give me a glass of cider?" and says he:

"I don't care if I do."

So he took and laid 'em on the shelf again and poured out a glass of cider. I took the glass of cider and drinkt it down, and, to tell you the truth about it, it was capital good cider. Then says I:

"I guess it's about time for me to be a-going," and so I stept along toward the door; but he ups and says, says he:

"Stop, mister, I believe you haven't paid me for the cider."

"Not paid you for the cider!" says I; "what do you mean by that? Didn't the biscuits that I give you just come to the cider?"

"Oh, ah, right!" says he.

So I started to go again, but before I had reached the door he says, says he:

"But stop, mister, you didn't pay me for the biscuits."

"What!" says I, "do you mean to impose upon me? Do you think I am going to pay you for the biscuits, and let you keep them, too? Ain't they there now on your shelf? What more do you want? I guess, sir, you don't whittle me in that way."

So I turned about and marched off and left the feller staring and scratching his head as tho' he was struck with a dunderment.

Howsomever, I didn't want to cheat him, only jest to show 'em it wasn't so easy a matter to pull my eye-teeth out; so I called in next day and paid him two cents.

William Cullen Bryant
THE MOSQUITO

Fair insect! that with threadlike legs spread out
  And blood-extracting bill and filmy wing,
Dost murmur, as thou slowly sail'st about,
  In pitiless ears, full many a plaintive thing,
And tell how little our large veins should bleed,
Would we but yield them to thy bitter need?

Unwillingly I own, and, what is worse,
  Full angrily men hearken to thy plaint;
Thou gettest many a brush and many a curse,
  For saying thou art gaunt and starved and faint.
Even the old beggar, while he asks for food,
Would kill thee, hapless stranger, if he could.

I call thee stranger, for the town, I ween,
  Has not the honor of so proud a birth-
Thou com'st from Jersey meadows, fresh and green,
  The offspring of the gods, though born on earth;
For Titan was thy sire, and fair was she,
The ocean nymph that nursed thy infancy.

Beneath the rushes was thy cradle swung,
  And when at length thy gauzy wings grew strong,
Abroad to gentle airs their folds were flung,

Rose in the sky, and bore thee soft along;
The south wind breathed to waft thee on thy way,
And danced and shone beneath the billowy bay.

Calm rose afar the city spires, and thence
    Came the deep murmur of its throng of men,
And as its grateful odors met thy sense,
    They seemed the perfumes of thy native fen.
Fair lay its crowded streets, and at the sight
Thy tiny song grew shriller with delight.

At length thy pinion fluttered in Broadway--
    Ah, there were fairy steps, and white necks kissed
By wanton airs, and eyes whose killing ray
    Shone through the snowy veils like stars through mist;
And fresh as morn, on many a cheek and chin,
Bloomed the bright blood through the transparent skin.

Sure these were sights to tempt an anchorite!
    What! do I hear thy slender voice complain?
Thou wailest when I talk of beauty's light,
    As if it brought the memory of pain.
Thou art a wayward being--well--come near,
And pour thy tale of sorrow in mine ear.

What say'st thou, slanderer! rouge makes thee sick?
    And China Bloom at best is sorry food?
And Rowland's Kalydor, if laid on thick,
    Poisons the thirsty wretch that bores for blood.
Go! 'Twas a just reward that met thy crime-
But shun the sacrilege another time.

That bloom was made to look at--not to touch;

To worship--not approach--that radiant white;
And well might sudden vengeance light on such
  As dared, like thee, most impiously to bite.
Thou shouldst have gazed at distance and admired-
Murmur'd thy admiration and retired.

Thou'rt welcome to the town--but why come here
  To bleed a brother poet, gaunt like thee?
Alas! the little blood I have is dear,
  And thin will be the banquet drawn from me.
Look round--the pale-eyed sisters in my cell,
Thy old acquaintance, Song and Famine, dwell.

Try some plump alderman, and suck the blood
  Enrich'd by gen'rous wine and costly meat;
On well-filled skins, sleek as thy native mud,
  Fix thy light pump, and press thy freckled feet.
Go to the men for whom, in ocean's halls,
The oyster breeds and the green turtle sprawls.

There corks are drawn, and the red vintage flows.
  To fill the swelling veins for thee, and now
The ruddy cheek, and now the ruddier nose
  Shall tempt thee, as thou flittest round the brow;
And when the hour of sleep its quiet brings,
No angry hand shall rise to brush thy wings.

John Carver
COUNTRY BURIAL-PLACES

In passing through New England, a stranger will be struck with the variety, in taste and feeling, respecting burial-places. Here and there may be seen a solitary grave, in a desolate and dreary pasture lot, and anon under the shade of some lone tree, the simple stone reared by affection to the memory of one known and loved by the humble fireside only. There, on that gentle elevation, sloping green and beautiful toward the south, is a family enclosure adorned with trees and filled with the graves of the household. How many breaking hearts have there left the loved till that bright morning! Here in this garden, beside the vine-covered arbor and amidst the shrubbery which her own hand planted, is the monument to the faithful wife and loving mother. How appropriate! How beautiful! And to the old landholders of New England, what motive to hold sacred from the hand of lucre so strong as the ground loved by the living as the burial- place of *their* dead!

Apropos to burying in gardens, I heard a story of an old man who was bent on interring his wife in his garden, despite of the opposition of all his neighbors to his doing so. Indeed, the old fellow avowed this as his chief reason and to all their entreaties and deprecations and earnest requests he still declared he would do it. Finding everything they could do to be of no avail, the people bethought themselves of a certain physician, who was said to have great influence over the old man, and who owned an orchard adjoining the very garden; so, going to him in a body, they besought him to attempt to change the determination of his obstinate friend. The doctor consented to do so and went. After offering his condolence on the loss of his wife, and proffering any aid he might be able to render at the funeral, the doctor said, "I understand you intend to bury your deceased wife in your garden."

"Yes," answered the old man, "I do. And the more people object the more I'm determined to do it!"

"Right!" replied the doctor, with an emphatic shake of the head, "Right! I applaud the deed. I'd bury her there, if I was you. The boys are always stealing the pears from my favorite tree that overhangs your garden, and by and by you'll die, Uncle Diddie, and they'll bury you there, too, and then I'm sure that the boys will never dare steal another pear."

"No! I'll be hanged if I bury her there," said the old man in great wrath. "I'll bury her in the graveyard."

New England can boast her beautiful places of sculpture, but as a common thing they are too much neglected, and attractive only to the lover of oddities and curious old epitaphs. Occasionally you may see a strangely shaped tomb, or as in a well-known village, a knocker placed on the door of his family vault by some odd specimen of humanity. When asked the reason for doing so singular a thing, he gravely replied that "when the old gentleman should come to claim his own, the tenants might have the pleasure of saying, 'not at home,' or of fleeing out of the back door."

In passing through these neglected grounds you will often find some touchingly beautiful scriptural allusion--some apt quotation or some emblem so lovely and instructive that the memory of it will go with you for days. Here in a neglected spot and amid a cluster of raised stones is the grave of the stranger clergyman's child, who died on its journey. The inscription is sweet when taken in connection with the portion of sacred history from which the quotation is made: "Is it well with the child? And she answered, It is well." Again, the only inscription is an emblem--a butterfly rising from the chrysalis. Glorious thought, embodied in emblem so singular! "Sown in corruption, raised in incorruption!"

Then come you to some strangely odd, as for instance:

"Here lies John Auricular,
  Who in the ways of the Lord walked perpendicular"

Again:

"Many a cold wind o'er my body shall roll

While in Abraham's bosom I'm feasting my soul"

appropriate certainly, as the grave was on a cold northeast slope of one of our bleak hills. Again, a Dutchman's epitaph for his twin babes:

"Here lies two babes, dead as two nits,
Who shook to death mit ague fits.
They was too good to live mit me.
So God He took 'em to live mit He."

There is the grave of a young man who, dying suddenly, was eulogized with this strange aim at the sublime:

"He lived,
He died!"

Not a hundred miles from Boston is a gravestone the epitaph upon which, to all who knew the parties, borders strongly upon the burlesque. A widower who within a few months buried his wife and adopted daughter, the former of whom was all her life long a thorn in his flesh, and whose death could not but have been a relief, wrote thus: "They were lovely and beloved in their lives, and in death were not divided." Poor man! Well *he* knew how full of strife and sorrow an evil woman can make life! He was worn to a shadow before her death, and his hair was all gone. Many of the neighbors thought surely that *he* well knew what had become of it, especially as it disappeared by the handful. But the grave covers all faults; and those who knew her could only hope that she might rest from her labors and her works follow her!

On a low, sandy mound far down on the Cape rises a tall slate stone, with fitting emblems and epitaphs as follows:

"Here lies Judy and John
That lovely pair,

John was killed by a whale,
And Judy sleeps here."

--Sketches of New England.

Danforth Marble
THE HOOSIER AND THE SALT-PILE

I'm sorry," says Dan, as he knocked the ashes from his regalia, as he sat in a small crowd over a glass of sherry at Florence's, New York, one evening. "I'm sorry that the stages are disappearing so rapidly; I never enjoyed traveling so well as in the slow coaches. I've made a good many passages over the Alleghanies, and across Ohio, from Cleveland to Columbus and Cincinnati, all over the South, down East, and up North, in stages, and I generally had a good time.

"When I passed over from Cleveland to Cincinnati, the last time, in a stage, I met a queer crowd--such a *corps*, such a time you never did see; I never was better amused in my life. We had a good team-- spanking horses, fine coaches, and one of them *drivers* you read of. Well, there was nine 'insiders,' and I don't believe there ever was a stageful of Christians ever started before so chuck full of music.

"There was a beautiful young lady going to one of the Cincinnati academies; next to her sat a Jew peddler--for Cowes and a market; wedging him in was a dandy blackleg, with jewelry and chains around his breast and neck--enough to hang him. There was myself and an old gentleman with large spectacles, gold-headed cane, and a jolly, soldiering-iron-looking nose; by him was a circus rider whose breath was enough to breed yaller fever and could be felt just as easy as cotton velvet! A cross old woman came next, and whose *look* would have given any reasonable man the double-breasted blues before breakfast; alongside of her was a rale backwoods preacher, with the biggest and ugliest mouth ever got up since the flood. He was flanked by the low comedian of the party, an Indiana Hoosier, 'gwine down to Orleans to get an army contract' to supply the forces then in Mexico with beef.

"We rolled along for some time; nobody seemed inclined to 'open.' The old aunty sot bolt upright, looking crab-apples and persimmons at the Hoosier and the preacher; the young lady dropped the green curtain of her bonnet over her pretty face, and leaned back in her seat, to nod and dream over japonicas and jumbles, pantalettes and poetry; the old gentleman, proprietor of the Bardolph 'nose,' looked out at the 'corduroy' and swashes; the gambler fell off into a doze, and the circus covey followed suit, leaving the preacher and me *vis-a-vis* and saying nothing to nobody. 'Indiany,' he stuck his mug out at the window and criticized the cattle we now and then passed. I was wishing somebody would give the conversation a start, when 'Indiany' made a break:

"'This ain't no great stock country,' says he to the old gentleman with the cane.

"'No, sir,' was the reply. 'There's very little grazing here; the range is nearly wore out.'

"Then there was nothing said again for some time. Bimeby the Hoosier opened again:

"'It's the d----est place for 'simmon trees and turkey buzzards I ever did see!'

"The old gentleman with the cane didn't say nothing, and the preacher gave a long groan. The young lady smiled through her veil, and the old lady snapped her eyes and looked sideways at the speaker.

"'Don't make much beef here, I reckon,' says the Hoosier.

"'No,' says the gentleman.

"'Well, I don't see how in h-ll they all manage to get along in a country whar thar ain't no ranges and they don't make no beef. A man ain't considered worth a cuss in Indiany what hasn't got his brand on a hundred head.'

"'Yours is a great beef country, I believe,' says the old gentleman.

"'Well, sir, it ain't anything else. A man that's got sense enuff to foller his own cow-bell with us ain't in no danger of starvin'. I'm gwine down to Orleans to see if I can't git a contract out of Uncle Sam to feed the boys what's been lickin' them infernal Mexicans so bad. I s'pose you've seed them cussed lies what's been in the papers about the Indiany boys at Bony Visty.'

"'I've read some accounts of the battle,' says the old gentleman, `that didn't give a very flattering account of the conduct of some of our troops.'

"With that the Indiany man went into a full explanation of the affair, and, gittin' warmed up as he went along, begun to cuss and swear like he'd been through a dozen campaigns himself. The old preacher listened to him with evident signs of displeasure, twistin' and groanin' till he couldn't stand it no longer.

"'My friend,' says he, 'you must excuse me, but your conversation would be a great deal more interesting to me--and I'm sure would please the company much better--if you wouldn't swear so terribly. It's very wrong to swear and I hope you'll have respect for our feelings if you hain't no respect for your Maker.'

"If the Hoosier had been struck with thunder and lightnin' he couldn't have been more completely tuck a-back. He shut his mouth right in the middle of what he was sayin' and looked at the preacher, while his face got as red as fire.

"'Swearin',' says the preacher, 'is a terrible bad practice, and there ain't no use in it nohow. The Bible says, "swear not at all," and I s'pose you know the Commandments about swearin'?'

"The old lady sort of brightened up--the preacher was her `duck of a man'; the old fellow with the `nose' and cane let off a few `umph, ah! umphs.' But 'Indiany' kept shady; he appeared to be *cowed* down.

"'I know,' says the preacher, 'that a great many people swear without thinkin', and some people don't believe the Bible.'

"And then he went on to preach a regular sermon agin swearing, and to quote Scripture like he had the whole Bible by heart. In the course of his argument he undertook to prove the Scriptures to be true, and told us all about the miracles and prophecies, and their fulfilment. The old gentleman with the cane took a part in the conversation, and the Hoosier listened without ever opening his head.

"'I've just heard of a gentleman,' says the preacher, 'that's been to the Holy Land and went over the Bible country. It's astonishin' to hear what wonderful things he has seen. He was at Sodom and Gomorrow, and seen the place whar Lot's wife fell!'

"'Ah,' says the old gentleman with the cane.

"'Yes,' says the preacher, 'he went to the very spot; and what's the remarkablest thing of all, he seen the pillar of salt what she was turned into!'

"'Is it possible!' says the old gentleman.

"'Yes, sir; he seen the salt, standin' thar to this day.'

"'What!' says the Hoosier,'real genewine, good salt?'

"'Yes, sir; a pillar of salt, jest as it was when that wicked woman was punished for her disobedience.'

"All but the gambler, who was snoozing in the corner of the coach, looked at the preacher--the Hoosier with an expression of countenance that plainly told that his mind was powerfully convicted of an important fact.

"'Right out in the open air?' he asked.

"'Yes, standin' right in the open field, whar she fell.'

"'Well, sir,' says 'Indiany,' 'all I've got to say is, *if she'd dropped in our parts, the cattle would have licked her up afore sundown!*'

"The preacher raised both his hands at such an irreverent remark, and the old gentleman laughed himself into a fit of asthmatics; what he didn't get over till he came to the next change of horses. The Hoosier had played the mischief with the gravity of the whole party; even the old maid had to put her handkerchief to her face, and the young lady's eyes were filled with tears for half an hour afterward. The old preacher hadn't another word to say on the subject; but whenever we came to any place or met anybody on the road, the circus man cursed the thing along by asking what was the price of salt."

Anne Bache
THE QUILTING

The day is set, the ladies met,
   And at the frame are seated;
In order plac'd, they work in haste,
   To get the quilt completed.
While fingers fly, their tongues they ply,
   And animate their labors,
By counting beaux, discussing clothes,
   Or talking of their neighbors.

"Dear, what a pretty frock you've on--"
   "I'm very glad you like it."
"I'm told that Miss Micomicon
   Don't speak to Mr. Micat."
"I saw Miss Bell the other day,
   Young Green's new gig adorning--"
"What keeps your sister Ann away?"
   "She went to town this morning."

"'Tis time to roll"--"my needle's broke--"
   "So Martin's stock is selling;"-
"Louisa's wedding-gown's bespoke--"
   "Lend me your scissors, Ellen."
"That match will never come about--"
   "Now don't fly in a passion;"

"Hair-puffs, they say, are going out--"
　"Yes, curls are all in fashion."

The quilt is done, the tea begun-
　The beaux are all collecting;
The table's cleared, the music heard-
　His partner each selecting.
The merry band in order stand,
　The dance begins with vigor;
And rapid feet the measure beat,
　And trip the mazy figure.

Unheeded fly the moments by,
　Old Time himself seems dancing,
Till night's dull eye is op'd to spy
　The steps of morn advancing.
Then closely stowed, to each abode,
　The carriages go tilting;
And many a dream has for its theme
　The pleasures of the Quilting.

Fitz-Greene Halleck
A FRAGMENT

His shop is a grocer's--a snug, genteel place,
    Near the corner of Oak Street and Pearl;
He can dress, dance, and bow to the ladies with grace,
    And ties his cravat with a curl.

He's asked to all parties--north, south, east and west,
    That take place between Chatham and Cherry,
And when he's been absent full oft has the "best
    Society" ceased to be merry.

And nothing has darkened a sky so serene,
    Nor disordered his beauship's Elysium,
Till this season among our elite there has been
    What is called by the clergy "a schism."

'Tis all about eating and drinking--one set
    Gives sponge-cake, a few kisses or so,
And is cooled after dancing with classic sherbet
    "Sublimed" [see Lord Byron] "with snow."

Another insists upon punch and perdrix,
    Lobster salad, champagne, and, by way
Of a novelty only, those pearls of our sea,
    Stewed oysters from Lynn-Haven Bay.

Miss Flounce, the young milliner, blue-eyed and bright,
   In the front parlor over her shop,
"Entertains," as the phrase is, a party to-night
   Upon peanuts and ginger pop.

And Miss Fleece, who's a hosier and not quite as young,
   But is wealthier far than Miss Flounce,
She "entertains" also to-night, with cold tongue,
   Smoked herring and cherry bounce.

In praise of cold water the Theban bard spoke,
   He of Teos sang sweetly of wine;
Miss Flounce is a Pindar in cashmere and cloak,
   Miss Fleece an Anacreon divine.

The Montagues carry the day in Swamp Place,
   In Pike Street the Capulets reign;
A limonadiere is the badge of one race,
   Of the other a flask of champagne.

Now as each the same evening her soiree announces,
   What better, he asks, can be done,
Than drink water from eight until ten with the Flounces,
   And then wine with the Fleeces till one!

DOMESTIC HAPPINESS

"Beside the nuptial curtain bright,"
  The Bard of Eden sings;
"Young Love his constant lamp will light
  And wave his purple wings."
But raindrops from the clouds of care
  May bid that lamp be dim,
And the boy Love will pout and swear,
  'Tis then no place for him.

So mused the lovely Mrs. Dash;
  'Tis wrong to mention names;
When for her surly husband's cash
  She urged in vain her claims.
"I want a little money, dear,
  For Vandervoort and Flandin,
Their bill, which now has run a year,
  To-morrow mean to hand in."

"More?" cried the husband, half asleep,
  "You'll drive me to despair";
The lady was too proud to weep,
  And too polite to swear.
She bit her lip for very spite,
  He felt a storm was brewing,
And dream'd of nothing else all night,

But brokers, banks, and ruin.

He thought her pretty once, but dreams
 Have sure a wondrous power,
For to his eye the lady seems
 Quite alter'd since that hour;
And Love, who on their bridal eve,
 Had promised long to stay;
Forgot his promise, took French leave,
 And bore his lamp away.

Charles F. Browne ("Artemus Ward")
ONE OF MR. WARD'S BUSINESS LETTERS

To the Editor of the--

Sir: I'm movin along--slowly along--down tords your place. I want you should rite me a letter, saying how is the show bizness in your place. My show at present consists of three moral Bares, a Kangaroo (a amoozin little Raskal--'twould make you larf yourself to deth to see the little cuss jump up and squeal), wax figgers of G. Washington, Gen. Tayler, John Bunyan, Capt. Kidd, and Dr. Webster in the act of killin Dr. Parkman, besides several miscellanyus moral wax statoots of celebrated piruts & murderers, &c., ekalled by few & exceld by none. Now, Mr. Editor, scratch orf a few lines sayin how is the show bizniss down to your place. I shall hav my hanbills dun at your offiss. Depend upon it. I want you should git my hanbills up in flamin stile. Also git up a tremenjus excitemunt in yr. paper 'bowt my onparaleled Show. We must fetch the public sumhow. We must wurk on their feelins. Cum the moral on em strong. If it's a temperance community, tell em I sined the pledge fifteen minits arter Ise born, but on the contery, ef your peple take their tods, say Mister Ward is as Jenial a feller as ever we met. full of conwiviality, & the life an sole of the Soshul Bored. Take, don't you? If you say anythin abowt my show, say my snaiks is as harmliss as the new born Babe. What a interistin study it is to see a zewological animil like a snake under perfect subjecshun! My kangaroo is the most larfable little cuss I ever saw. All for 15 cents. I am anxyus to skewer your inflooence. I repeet in regard to them hanbills that I shall git 'em struck orf up to your printin office. My perlitical sentiments agree with yourn exactly. I know they do, becaws I never saw a man whoos didn't.

Respectively yures, A. WARD.

P.S.--You scratch my back & Ile scratch your back.

ON "FORTS"

Every man has got a Fort. It's sum men's fort to do one thing, and some other men's fort to do another, while there is numeris shiftliss critters goin' round loose whose fort is not to do nothin'.

Shakspeer rote good plase, but he wouldn't hav succeeded as a Washington correspondent of a New York daily paper. He lackt the rekesit fancy and immagginashun.

That's so!

Old George Washington's Fort was not to hev eny public man of the present day resemble him to eny alarmin extent. Whare bowts can George's ekal be found? I ask, & boldly answer no whares, or any whare else.

Old man Townsin's Fort was to maik Sassy-periller. "Goy to the world! anuther life saived!" (Cotashun from Townsin's advertisement.)

Cyrus Field's Fort is to lay a sub-machine tellegraf under the boundin billers of the Oshun and then have it Bust.

Spaldin's Fort is to maik Prepared Gloo, which mends everything. Wonder ef it will mend a sinner's wickid waze. (Impromptoo goak.)

Zoary's Fort is to be a femaile circus feller.

My Fort is the grate moral show bizniss & ritin choice famerly literatoor for the noospapers. That's what's the matter with *me*.

&., &., &. So I mite go on to a indefnit extent.

Twict I've endevered to do things which thay wasn't my Fort. The fust time was when I undertuk to lick a owdashus cuss who cut a hole in my tent & krawld threw. Sez I, "My jentle Sir, go out or I shall fall on to you putty hevy." Sez he, "Wade in, Old wax figgers," whereupon I went for him, but he cawt me powerful on the hed & knockt me threw the tent into a cow pastur. He pursood the attack & flung me into a mud puddle. As I arose & rung out my drencht garmints I koncluded fitin wasn't my Fort. He now rize the kurtin upon Seen 2nd: It is rarely seldum that I seek consolation in the Flowin Bole. But in a certain town in Injianny in the Faul of 18--, my orgin grinder got sick with the fever & died. I never felt so ashamed in my life, & I thowt I'd hist in a few swallers of suthin strengthnin. Konsequents was I histid in so much I didn't zackly know whare bowts I was. I turned my livin wild beasts of Pray loose into the streets and spilt all my wax wurks. I then bet I cood play hoss. So I hitched myself to a Kanawl bote, there bein two other hosses hicht on also, one behind and another ahead of me. The driver hollerd for us to git up, and we did. But the hosses bein onused to sich a arrangemunt begun to kick & squeal and rair up. Konsequents was I was kickt vilently in the stummuck & back, and presuntly I fownd myself in the Kanawl with the other hosses, kickin & yellin like a tribe of Cusscaroorus savvijis. I was rescood & as I was bein carrid to the tavern on a hemlock Bored I sed in a feeble voise, "Boys, playin hoss isn't my Fort."

Morul.--Never don't do nothin which isn't your Fort, for ef you do you'll find yourself splashin round in the Kanawl, figgeratively speakin.

James Russell Lowell
WITHOUT AND WITHIN

My coachman, in the moonlight there,
  Looks through the sidelight of the door;
I hear him with his brethren swear,
  As I could do--but only more.

Flattening his nose against the pane,
  He envies me my brilliant lot,
Breathes on his aching fist in vain,
  And dooms me to a place more hot.

He sees me into supper go,
  A silken wonder at my side,
Bare arms, bare shoulders, and a row
  Of flounces, for the door too wide.

He thinks how happy is my arm,
  'Neath its white-gloved and jeweled load;
And wishes me some dreadful harm,
  Hearing the merry corks explode.

Meanwhile I inly curse the bore
  Of hunting still the same old coon,
And envy him, outside the door,
  The golden quiet of the moon.

The winter wind is not so cold
  As the bright smile he sees me win,
Nor the host's oldest wine so old
  As our poor gabble, sour and thin.

I envy him the rugged prance
  By which his freezing feet he warms,
And drag my lady's chains and dance,
  The galley-slave of dreary forms.

Oh, could he have my share of din,
  And I his quiet--past a doubt
'Twould still be one man bored within,
  And just another bored without.

Louisa May Alcott
STREET SCENES IN WASHINGTON

The mules were my especial delight; and an hour's study of a constant succession of them introduced me to many of their characteristics: for six of these odd little beasts drew each army wagon and went hopping like frogs through the stream of mud that gently rolled along the street. The coquettish mule had small feet, a nicely trimmed tassel of a tail, perked-up ears, and seemed much given to little tosses of the head, affected skips and prances; and, if he wore the bells or were bedizened with a bit of finery, put on as many airs as any belle. The moral mule was a stout, hard-working creature, always tugging with all his might, often pulling away after the rest had stopped, laboring under the conscientious delusion that food for the entire army depended upon his private exertions. I respected this style of mule; and, had I possessed a juicy cabbage, would have pressed it upon him with thanks for his excellent example. The histrionic mule was a melodramatic quadruped, prone to startling humanity by erratic leaps and wild plunges, much shaking of his stubborn head, and lashing out of his vicious heels; now and then falling flat and apparently dying a la Forrest; a gasp--a squirm--a flop, and so on, till the street was well blocked up, the drivers all swearing like demons in bad hats, and the chief actor's circulation decidedly quickened by every variety of kick, cuff, jerk and haul. When the last breath seemed to have left his body, and "doctors were in vain," a sudden resurrection took place; and if ever a mule laughed with scornful triumph, that was the beast, as he leisurely rose, gave a comfortable shake, and, calmly regarding the excited crowd, seemed to say--"A hit! a decided hit! for the stupidest of animals has bamboozled a dozen men. Now, then! what are *you* stopping the way for?" The pathetic mule was, perhaps, the most interesting of all; for, though he always seemed to be the smallest, thinnest, weakest of the six, the postillion with big boots, long- tailed coat and heavy whip was sure to bestride this one, who struggled feebly along, head down, coat muddy and rough, eye spiritless and sad, his very tail a mortified stump, and the whole beast a picture of meek misery, fit to touch a heart of stone. The jovial mule was a roly-poly, happy-go-lucky little piece of horseflesh, taking everything easily, from cudgeling to caressing; strolling along with a roguish twinkle of the eye, and, if the thing were possible, would have had his hands in his pockets and whistled as he went. If there ever chanced to be an apple core, a stray turnip or wisp of hay in the gutter, this Mark Tapley was sure to find it, and none of his mates seemed to begrudge him his bite. I suspected this fellow was the peacemaker, confidant and friend of all the others, for he had a sort of "Cheer-up-old-boy-I'll-pull-you-through" look which was exceedingly engaging.

Pigs also possessed attractions for me, never having had an opportunity of observing their graces of mind and manner till I came to Washington, whose porcine citizens appeared to enjoy a larger liberty than many of its human ones. Stout, sedate-looking pigs hurried by each morning to their places of business, with a preoccupied air, and sonorous greetings to their friends. Genteel pigs, with an extra curl to their tails, promenaded in pairs, lunching here and there, like gentlemen of leisure. Rowdy pigs pushed the passersby off the sidewalk; tipsy pigs hiccoughed their version of "We won't go home till morning" from the gutter; and delicate young pigs tripped daintily through the mud as if they plumed themselves upon their ankles, and kept themselves particularly neat in point of stockings. Maternal pigs, with their interesting families, strolled by in the sun; and often the pink, baby-like squealers lay down for a nap, with a trust in Providence worthy of human imitation.--Hospital Sketches.

MIS' SMITH

All day she hurried to get through, The same as lots of wimmin do; Sometimes at night her husban' said, "Ma, ain't you goin' to come to bed?" And then she'd kinder give a hitch, And pause half way between a stitch, And sorter sigh, and say that she Was ready as she'd ever be, She reckoned.

And so the years went one by one, An' somehow she was never done; An' when the angel said, as how "Miss Smith, it's time you rested now," She sorter raised her eyes to look A second, as a stitch she took; "All right, I'm comin' now," says she, "I'm ready as I'll ever be, I reckon."

Albert Bigelow Paine.
A BOSTON LULLABY

Baby's brain is tired of thinking
  On the Wherefore and the Whence;
Baby's precious eyes are blinking
  With incipient somnolence.
Little hands are weary turning
  Heavy leaves of lexicon;
Little nose is fretted learning
  How to keep its glasses on.
Baby knows the laws of nature
  Are beneficent and wise;
His medulla oblongata
  Bids my darling close his eyes
And his pneumogastrics tell him
  Quietude is always best
When his little cerebellum
  Needs recuperative rest.
Baby must have relaxation,
  Let the world go wrong or right-
Sleep, my darling, leave Creation
  To its chances for the night.

James Jeffrey Roche.

IRISH ASTRONOMY

O'Ryan was a man of might
   Whin Ireland was a nation,
But poachin' was his heart's delight
   And constant occupation.
He had an ould militia gun,
   And sartin sure his aim was;
He gave the keepers many a run,
   And wouldn't mind the game laws

St. Pathrick wanst was passin' by
   O'Ryan's little houldin',
And, as the saint felt wake and dhry
   He thought he'd enther bould in.
"O'Ryan," says the saint, "avick!
   To praich at Thurles I'm goin';
So let me have a rasher quick,
   And a dhrop of Innishowen."

"No rasher will I cook for you
   While betther is to spare, sir,
But here's a jug of mountain dew,
   And there's a rattlin' hare, sir."
St. Pathrick he looked mighty sweet,
   And says he, "Good luck attind you,
And whin you're in your windin' sheet,

It's up to heaven I'll sind you."

O'Ryan gave his pipe a whiff-
  "Them tidin's is thransportin',
But may I ax your saintship if
  There's any kind of sportin'?"
St. Pathrick said, "A Lion's there,
  Two Bears, a Bull, and Cancer"-
"Bedad," says Mick, "the huntin's rare;
  St. Pathrick, I'm your man, sir."

So, to conclude my song aright,
  For fear I'd tire your patience
You'll see O'Ryan any night,
  Amid the constellations.
And Venus follows in his track
  Till Mars grows jealous raally,
But, faith, he fears the Irish knack
  Of handling the shillaly.

Charles Graham Halpine.

BESSIE BROWN, M.D.

'Twas April when she came to town;
   The birds had come, the bees were swarming.
Her name, she said, was Doctor Brown:
   I saw at once that she was charming.
She took a cottage tinted green,
   Where dewy roses loved to mingle;
And on the door, next day, was seen
   A dainty little shingle.

Her hair was like an amber wreath;
   Her hat was darker, to enhance it.
The violet eyes that glowed beneath
   Were brighter than her keenest lancet.
The beauties of her glove and gown
   The sweetest rhyme would fail to utter.
Ere she had been a day in town
   The town was in a flutter.

The gallants viewed her feet and hands,
   And swore they never saw such wee things;
The gossips met in purring bands
   And tore her piecemeal o'er the tea things.
The former drank the Doctor's health
   With clinking cups, the gay carousers;
The latter watched her door by stealth,

Just like so many mousers.

But Doctor Bessie went her way
  Unmindful of the spiteful cronies,
And drove her buggy every day
  Behind a dashing pair of ponies.
Her flower-like face so bright she bore
  I hoped that time might never wilt her.
The way she tripped across the floor
  Was better than a philter.

Her patients thronged the village street;
  Her snowy slate was always quite full.
Some said her bitters tasted sweet,
  And some pronounced her pills delightful.
'Twas strange--I knew not what it meant-
  She seemed a nymph from Eldorado;
Where'er she came, where'er she went,
  Grief lost its gloomy shadow.

Like all the rest, I, too, grew ill;
  My aching heart there was no quelling.
I tremble at my Doctor's bill-
  And lo! the items still are swelling.
The drugs I've drunk you'd weep to hear!
  They've quite enriched the fair concocter,
And I'm a ruined man, I fear,
  Unless--I wed the Doctor!

Samuel Minturn Peck.

THE TROUT, THE CAT AND THE FOX
A Fable

(Anonymous)

A fine full-grown Trout for had some time kept his station in a clear stream, when, one morning, a Cat, extravagantly fond, as cats are wont to be, of fish, caught a glimpse of him, as he glided from beneath an overhanging part of the bank, toward the middle of the river; and with this glimpse, she resolved to spare no pains to capture him. As she sat on the bank waiting for the return of the fish, and laying a plan for her enterprise, a Fox came up, and saluting her, said:

"Your servant, Mrs. Puss. A pleasant place this for taking the morning air; and a notable place for fish, eh!"

"Good morning, Mr. Reynard," replied the Cat. "The place is, as you say, pleasant enough. As for fish, you can judge for yourself whether there are any in this part of the river. I do not deny that near the falls, about four miles from here, some very fine salmon and other fish are to be found."

At this very moment, very inappositely for the Cat's hint, the Trout made his appearance; and the Fox looking significantly at her, said:

"The falls, madam! Perhaps this fine Trout is on his way thither. It may be that you would like the walk; allow me the pleasure of accompanying you?"

"I thank you, sir," replied the Cat, "but I am not disposed to walk so far at present. Indeed, I hardly know whether I am quite well. I think I will rest myself a little, and then return home."

"Whatever you may determine," rejoined the Fox, "I hope to be permitted to

enjoy your society and conversation; and possibly I may have the great gratification of preventing the tedium which, were you left alone, your indisposition might
produce."

In speaking thus, the crafty Fox had no doubt that the only indisposition from
which the Cat was suffering was an unwillingness to allow him a share of her booty;
and he was determined that, so far as management could go, she should catch no
fish that day without his being a party to the transaction. As the trout still continued in sight, be began to commend his shape and color; and the Cat, seeing no way
of getting rid of him, finally agreed that they should jointly try their skill and divide
the spoil. Upon this compact, they both went actively to work.

They agreed first to try the following device: A small knob of earth covered
with rushes stood in the water close to the bank. Both the fishers were to crouch
behind these rushes; the Fox was to move the water very gently with the end of his
long brush, and withdraw it so soon as the Trout's attention should have been drawn
to that point; and the Cat was to hold her right paw underneath, and be ready, so
soon as the fish should come over it, to throw him out on the bank. No sooner was
the execution of this device commenced than it seemed likely to succeed. The Trout
soon noticed the movement on the water, and glided quickly toward the point
where it was made; but when he had arrived within about twice his own length of
it, he stopped and then backed toward the middle of the river. Several times this
maneuver was repeated, and always with the same result, until the tricky pair were
convinced that they must try some other scheme.

It so happened that whilst they were considering what they should do next,
the Fox espied a small piece of meat, when it was agreed that he should tear this
into little bits and throw them into the stream above where they then were; that
the Cat should wait, crouched behind a tuft of grass, to dash into the river and seize
the Trout, if he should come to take any piece of meat floating near the bank; and
that the Fox should, on the first movement of the Cat, return and give his help. This
scheme was put into practice, but with no better success than the other. The Trout
came and took the pieces of meat which had floated farthest off from the bank, but
to those which floated near he seemed to pay no attention. As he rose to take the
last, he put his mouth out of the water and said, "To other travelers with these petty
tricks: here we are 'wide awake as a black fish' and are not to be caught with bits

and scraps, like so many silly gudgeons!"

As the Trout went down, the Fox said, in an undertone: "Say you so, my fine fellow; we may, perhaps, make a ***gudgeon*** of you yet!"

Then, turning to the Cat, he proposed to her a new scheme in the following terms:

"I have a scheme to propose which cannot, I am persuaded, fail of succeeding, if you will lend your talent and skill for the execution of it. As I crossed the bridge, a little way above, I saw the dead body of a small dog, and near it a flat piece of wood rather longer than your person. Now, let us throw the dead dog into the river and give the Trout time to examine it; then, let us put the piece of wood into the water, and do you set yourself upon it so that it shall be lengthwise under you, and your mouth may lean over one edge and your tail hang in the water as if you were dead. The Trout, no doubt, will come up to you, when you may seize him and paddle to the bank with him, where I will be in waiting to help you land the prey."

The scheme pleased the Cat so much that, in spite of her repugnance to the wetting, which it promised her, she resolved to act the part which the cunning Fox had assigned to her. They first threw the dead dog into the river and, going down the stream, they soon had the satisfaction of seeing the Trout glide up close to it and examine it. They then returned to the bridge and put the piece of wood into the water, and the Cat, having placed herself upon it and taken a posture as if she were dead, was soon carried down by the current to where the Trout was. Apparently without the least suspicion, he came up close to the Cat's head, and she, seizing him by one of his gills, held him in spite of all his struggles. The task of regaining the bank still had to be performed, and this was no small difficulty, for the Trout struggled so hard, and the business of navigation was so new to the Cat, that not without great labor and fatigue did she reach the place where the Fox was waiting for her. As one end of the board struck the bank, the Fox put his right forepaw upon it, then seizing the fish near the tail, as the Cat let it go, he gave the board a violent push which sent it toward the middle of the stream, and instantly ran off with the Trout in his mouth toward the bridge.

It had so happened that after the Fox had quitted the bridge the last time, an Otter had come there to watch for fish, and he, seeing the Trout in the Fox's mouth, rushed toward him, and compelled him to drop the fish and put himself on the defensive. It had also happened that this Otter had been seen in an earlier part of the day, and that notice of him had been given to the farmer to whom the Cat belonged, and who had more than once declared that if ever he found her fishing again she should be thrown into the river with a stone tied to her neck. The moment the farmer heard of the Otter, he took his gun, and followed by a laborer and two strong dogs, went toward the river, where he arrived just as the Cat, exhausted by the fatigue of her second voyage, was crawling up the bank. Immediately he ordered the laborer to put the sentence of drowning in execution; then, followed by his dogs, he arrived near the bridge just as the Fox and the Otter were about to join battle. Instantly the dogs set on the Fox and tore him to pieces; and the farmer, shooting the Otter dead on the spot, possessed himself of the Trout, which had thus served to detain first one, then the other of his destroyers, till a severe punishment had overtaken each of them. Moral.--The inexperienced are never so much in danger of being deceived and hurt as when they think themselves a match for the crafty, and suppose that they have penetrated their designs and seen through all their stratagems. As to the crafty, they are ever in danger, either by being overreached one by another or of falling in a hurry into some snare of their own, where, as commonly happens, should they be caught, they are treated with a full measure of severity.--Aesop, Jr., in America.

Robert C. Sands
A MONODY

Made on the Late Mr. Samuel Patch, by an Aadmirer of the Bathos
By water he shall die and take his end.--Shakespeare

Toll for Sam Patch! Sam Patch, who jumps no more,
   This or the world to come. Sam Patch is dead!
The vulgar pathway to the unknown shore
    Of dark futurity, he would not tread.
    No friends stood sorrowing round his dying bed;
Nor with decorous woe, sedately stepp'd
    Behind his corpse, and tears by retail shed--
The mighty river, as it onward swept,
In one great wholesale sob, his body drowned and kept.

Toll for Sam Patch! he scorned the common way
    That leads to fame, up heights of rough ascent,
And having heard Pope and Longinus say
    That some great men had risen by falls, he went
    And jumped, where wild Passaic's waves had rent
The antique rocks--the air free passage gave--
    And graciously the liquid element
Upbore him, like some sea-god on its wave;
And all the people said that Sam was very brave.

Fame, the clear spirit that doth to heaven upraise,
   Let Sam to dive into what Byron calls
The hell of waters. For the sake of praise,
   He wooed the bathos down great waterfalls;
   The dizzy precipice, which the eye appals
Of travelers for pleasure, Samuel found
   Pleasant as are to women lighted halls,
Crammed full of fools and fiddles; to the sound
Of the eternal roar, he timed his desperate bound.

Sam was a fool. But the large world of such
   Has thousands--better taught, alike absurd,
And less sublime. Of fame he soon got much,
   Where distant cataracts spout, of him men heard.
   Alas for Sam! Had he aright preferred
The kindly element, to which he gave
   Himself so fearlessly, we had not heard
That it was now his winding sheet and grave,
Nor sung, 'twixt tears and smiles, our requiem for the brave.

He soon got drunk with rum and with renown,
   As many others in high places do--
Whose fall is like Sam's last--for down and down,
   By one mad impulse driven, they flounder through
   The gulf that keeps the future from our view,
And then are found not. May they rest in peace!
   We heave the sigh to human frailty due--
And shall not Sam have his? The muse shall cease
To keep the heroic roll, which she began in Greece--

With demigods who went to the Black Sea
   For wool (and if the best accounts be straight,
Came back, in Negro phraseology,

With the same wool each upon his pate),
　In which she chronicled the deathless fate
Of him who jumped into the perilous ditch
　Left by Rome's street commissioners, in a state
Which made it dangerous, and by jumping which
He made himself renowned and the contractors rich--

I say the muse shall quite forget to sound
　The chord whose music is undying, if
She do not strike it when Sam Patch is drowned.
　Leander dived for love. Leucadia's cliff
　The Lesbian Sappho leapt from in a miff,
To punish Phaon; Icarus went dead
　Because the wax did not continue stiff;
And, had he minded what his father said,
He had not given a name unto his watery bed.

And Helle's case was all an accident,
　As everybody knows. Why sing of these?
Nor would I rank with Sam that man who went
　Down into Aetna's womb--Empedocles,
　I think he called himself. Themselves to please,
Or else unwillingly, they made their springs;
　For glory in the abstract, Sam made his,
To prove to all men, commons, lords, and kings,
That "some things may be done, as well as other things."

I will not be fatigued, by citing more
　Who jump'd of old, by hazard or design,
Nor plague the weary ghosts of boyish lore,
　Vulcan, Apollo, Phaeton--in fine
　All Tooke's Pantheon. Yet they grew divine
By their long tumbles; and if we can match

Their hierarchy, shall we not entwine
One wreath? Who ever came "up to the scratch,"
And for so little, jumped so bravely as Sam Patch?

To long conclusions many men have jumped
  In logic, and the safer course they took;
By any other they would have been stumped,
  Unable to argue, or to quote a book,
  And quite dumbfounded, which they cannot brook;
They break no bones, and suffer no contusion,
  Hiding their woful fall, by hook and crook,
In slang and gibberish, sputtering and confusion;
But that was not the way Sam came to conclusion.

He jumped in person. Death or victory
  Was his device, "and there was no mistake,"
Except his last; and then he did but die,
  A blunder which the wisest men will make.
  Aloft, where mighty floods the mountains break,
To stand, the target of the thousand eyes,
  And down into the coil and water-quake,
To leap, like Maia's offspring, from the skies--
For this all vulgar flights he ventured to despise.

And while Niagara prolongs its thunder,
  Though still the rock primeval disappears
And nations change their bounds--the theme of wonder
  Shall Sam go down the cataract of long years:
  And if there be sublimity in tears,
Those shall be precious which the adventurer shed
  When his frail star gave way, and waked his fears,
Lest, by the ungenerous crowd it might be said,
That he was all a hoax, or that his pluck had fled.

Who would compare the maudlin Alexander,
   Blubbering because he had no job in hand,
Acting the hypocrite, or else the gander,
   With Sam, whose grief we all can understand?
   His crying was not womanish, nor plann'd
For exhibition; but his heart o'erswelled
   With its own agony, when he the grand,
Natural arrangements for a jump beheld.
And measuring the cascade, found not his courage quelled.

His last great failure set the final seal
   Unto the record Time shall never tear,
While bravery has its honor--while men feel
   The holy natural sympathies which are
   First, last and mightiest in the bosom. Where
The tortured tides of Genesee descend,
   He came--his only intimate a bear--
(We know now that he had another friend),
The martyr of renown, his wayward course to end.

The fiend that from the infernal rivers stole
   Hell-drafts for man, too much tormented him;
With nerves unstrung, but steadfast of his soul,
   He stood upon the salient current's brim;
   His head was giddy, and his sight was dim;
And then he knew this leap would be his last--
   Saw air, and earth, and water, wildly swim,
With eyes of many multitudes, dense and vast,
That stared in mockery; none a look of kindness cast.

Beat down, in the huge amphitheatre,
   "I see before me the gladiator lie,"
And tier on tier, the myriads waiting there

The bow of grace without one pitying eye--
   He was a slave--a captive hired to die--
was born free as Caesar; and he might
   The hopeless issue have refused to try;
No! with true leap, but soon with faltering flight--
"Deep in the roaring gulf, he plunged to endless night."

But, ere he leapt, he begged of those who made
   Money by this dread venture, that if he
Should perish, such collection should be paid
   As might be picked up from the "company"
   This, his last request, shall be--
Tho' she who bore him ne'er his fate should know--
   An iris, glittering o'er his memory--
When all the streams have worn their barriers low,
And, by the sea drunk up, forever cease to flow.

On him who chooses to jump down cataracts,
   Why should the sternest moralist be severe?
Judge not the dead by prejudice--but facts,
   Such as in strictest evidence appear.
   Else were the laurels of all ages sere.
Give to the brave, who have passed the final goal--
   The gates that ope not back--the generous tear;
And let the muse's clerk upon her scroll
In coarse, but honest verse, make up the judgment roll.

 that Sam Patch
   Shall never be forgot in prose or rhyme;
His name shall be a portion in the batch
   Of the heroic dough, which baking Time
   Kneads for consuming ages--and the chime
Of Fame's old bells, long as they truly ring,

Shall tell of him; he dived for the sublime,
And found it. Thou, who, with the eagle's wing,
Being a goose, would'st fly--dream not of such a thing!

THE BRITISH MATRON

(Anonymous)

I have heard a good deal of the tenacity with which English ladies retain their personal beauty to a late period of life; but (not to suggest that an American eye needs use and cultivation before it can quite appreciate the charm of English beauty at any age) it strikes me that an English lady of fifty is apt to become a creature less refined and delicate, so far as her physique goes, than anything that we Western people class under the name of woman. She has an awful ponderosity of frame--not pulpy, like the looser development of our few fat women, but massive, with solid beef and streaky tallow; so that (though struggling manfully against the ideal) you inevitably think of her as made up of steaks and sirloins. When she walks her advance is elephantine. When she sits down it is on a great round space of her Maker's footstool, where she looks as if nothing could ever move her. She imposes awe and respect by the muchness of her personality, to such a degree that you probably credit her with far greater moral and intellectual force than she can fairly claim. Her visage is usually grim and stern, seldom positively forbidding, yet calmly terrible, not merely by its breadth and weight of feature, but because it seems to express so much well-defined self-reliance, such acquaintance with the world, its toils, troubles and dangers, and such sturdy capacity for trampling down a foe. Without anything positively salient, or actively offensive, or, indeed, unjustly formidable to her neighbors, she has the effect of a seventy-four-gun ship in time of peace; for, while you assure yourself that there is no real danger, you cannot help thinking how tremendous would be her onset if pugnaciously inclined, and how futile the effort to inflict any counter-injury. She certainly looks tenfold--nay, a hundredfold-- better able to take care of herself than our slender-framed and haggard womankind; but I have not found reason to suppose that the English dowager of fifty has actually greater courage, fortitude and strength of character than our women of similar age, or even a tougher physical endurance than they. Morally, she is strong, I suspect, only in society and in common routine of social affairs, and would be found powerless and timid in any exceptional strait that might call for energy outside of the conventionalities amid which she has grown up.

You can meet this figure in the street, and live, and even smile at the recollection. But conceive of her in a ballroom, with the bare, brawny arms that she invariably displays there, and all the other corresponding development, such as is beautiful in the maiden blossom, but a spectacle to howl at in such an overblown cabbage-rose as this.

Yet, somewhere in this enormous bulk there must be hidden the modest, slender, violet-nature of a girl, whom an alien mass of earthliness has unkindly overgrown; for an English maiden in her teens, though very seldom so pretty as our own damsels, possesses, to say the truth, a certain charm of half-blossom, and delicately folded leaves, and tender womanhood, shielded by maidenly reserves, with which, somehow or other, our American girls often fail to adorn themselves during an appreciable moment. It is a pity that the English violet should grow into such an outrageously developed peony as I have attempted to describe. I wonder whether a middle-aged husband ought to be considered as legally married to all the accretions that have overgrown the slenderness of his bride, since he led her to the altar, and which make her so much more than he ever bargained for! Is it not a sounder view of the case that the matrimonial bond cannot be held to include the three-fourths of the wife that had no existence when the ceremony was performed? And ought not an English married pair to insist upon the celebration of a silver wedding at the end of twenty-five years to legalize all that corporeal growth of which both parties have individually come into possession since pronounced one flesh?--Our Old Home.

THE POSTER GIRL

The blessed Poster Girl leaned out
  From a pinky-purple heaven;
One eye was red and one was green;
  Her bang was cut uneven;
She had three fingers on her hand,
  And the hairs on her head were seven,

Her robe, ungirt from clasp to hem,
  No sunflowers did adorn;
But a heavy Turkish portiere
  Was very neatly worn;
And the hat that lay along her back
  Was yellow like canned corn.

It was a kind of wobbly wave
  That she was standing on,
And high aloft she flung a scarf
  That must have weighed a ton;
And she was rather tall--at least
  She reached up to the sun.

She curved and writhed, and then she said
  Less green of speech than blue:
"Perhaps I absurd--perhaps
  I appeal to you;

But my artistic worth depends
  Upon the point of view."

I saw her smile, although her eyes
  Were only smudgy smears;
And then she swished her swirling arms,
  And wagged her gorgeous ears,
She sobbed a blue-and-green-checked sob,
  And wept some purple tears.

Carolyn Wells.

James Gardner Sanderson
THE CONUNDRUM OF THE GOLF LINKS

(With thanks to Kipling)

When the flush of the new-born sun fell first on
  Eden's gold and green,
Our Father Adam sat under the Tree and shaved
  his driver clean,
And joyously whirled it round his head and
  knocked the apples off,
Till the Devil whispered behind the leaves:
  "Well done--but is it golf?"

Wherefore he called his wife and fled to practise
  again his swing--
The first of the world who foozled his stroke (yet
  the grandpapa of Tyng);
And he left his clubs to the use of his sons--and
  that was a glorious gain,
When the Devil chuckled "Beastly Golf" in the
  ear of the horrored Cain.

They putted and drove in the North and South;
  they talked and laid links in the West;
Till the waters rose o'er Ararat's tees, and the
  aching wrists could rest--

Could rest till that blank, blank canvasback,
   heard the Devil jeer and scoff,
As he flew with the flood-fed olive branch, "Dry
   weather. Let's play golf."

They pulled and sliced and pounded the earth,
   and the balls went sailing off
Into bunkers and trees while the Devil grinned,
   "Keep your eye on it! not golf."
Then the Devil took his sulphured cleik and
   mightily he swung,
While each man marveled and cursed his form
   and each in an alien tongue.

The tale is as old as the Eden Tree--and new as
   the newest green,
For each man knows ere his lip thatch grows the
   caddy's mocking mien.
And each man hears, though the ball falls fair,
   the Devil's cursed cough
Of joy as the man holes out in ten, "You did
   it--but what poor golf!"

We have learned to whittle the Eden Tree to
   the shape of a niblick's shaft,
We have learned to make a mashie with a
   wondrous handicraft,
We know that a hazard is often played best by
   re-driving off,
But the Devil whoops as he whooped of old, "It's
   easy, but is it golf?"

When the flicker of summer falls faint on the

Clubroom's gold and green,
The sons of Adam sit them down and boast of
   strokes unseen;
They talk of stymies and brassie lies to the tune
   of the steward's cough,
But the Devil whispers in their ears, "Gadzooks!
   But that's not golf!"

Now if we could win to the Eden Tree where
   the Nine-Mile Links are laid,
And seat ourselves where Man first swore as he
   drove from the grateful shade,
And if we could play where our Fathers played
   and follow our swings well through,
By the favor of God we might know of Golf
   what our Father Adam knew.

Harriet Beecher Stowe
THE MINISTER'S WOOING

Wal, the upshot on't was, they fussed and fuzzled and wuzzled till they'd drinked up all the tea in the teapot; and then they went down and called on the Parson, and wuzzled him all up talkin' about this, that, and t'other that wanted lookin' to, and that it was no way to leave everything to a young chit like Huldy, and that he ought to be lookin' about for an experienced woman.

"The Parson, he thanked 'em kindly, and said he believed their motives was good, but he didn't go no further.

"He didn't ask Mis' Pipperidge to come and stay there and help him, nor nothin' o' that kind; but he said he'd attend to matters himself. The fact was, the Parson had got such a likin' for havin' Huldy 'round that he couldn't think o' such a thing as swappin' her off for the Widder Pipperidge.

"'But,' he thought to himself, 'Huldy is a good girl; but I oughtn't to be a-leavin' everything to her--it's too hard on her. I ought to be instructin' and guidin' and helpin' of her; 'cause 'tain't everybody could be expected to know and do what Mis' Carryl did'; and so at it he went; and Lordy massy! didn't Huldy hev a time on't when the minister began to come out of his study and wanted to ten' 'round an' see to things? Huldy, you see, thought all the world of the minister, and she was 'most afraid to laugh; but she told me she couldn't, for the life of her, help it when his back was turned, for he wuzzled things up in the most singular way. But Huldy, she'd just say, 'Yes, sir,' and get him off into his study, and go on her own way.

"'Huldy,' says the minister one day, 'you ain't experienced outdoors; and when you want to know anything you must come to me.'

"'Yes, sir,' said Huldy.

"'Now, Huldy,' says the Parson, 'you must be sure to save the turkey eggs, so that we can have a lot of turkeys for Thanksgiving.'

"'Yes, sir,' says Huldy; and she opened the pantry door and showed him a nice dishful she'd been a-savin' up. Wal, the very next day the parson's hen-turkey was found killed up to old Jim Scrogg's barn. Folks say Scroggs killed it, though Scroggs, he stood to it he didn't; at any rate, the Scroggses they made a meal on't, and Huldy, she felt bad about it 'cause she'd set her heart on raisin' the turkeys; and says she, 'Oh, dear! I don't know what I shall do. I was just ready to set her.'

"'Do, Huldy?' says the Parson; 'why, there's the other turkey, out there by the door, and a fine bird, too, he is.'

"Sure enough, there was the old tom-turkey a-struttin' and a-sidlin' and a-quitterin', and a-floutin' his tail feathers in the sun, like a lively young widower all ready to begin life over again.

"'But,' says Huldy, 'you know *he* can't set on eggs.'

"'He can't? I'd like to know why" says the Parson. 'He *shall* set on eggs, and hatch 'em, too.'

"'Oh, Doctor!' says Huldy, all in a tremble; 'cause, you know, she didn't want to contradict the minister, and she was afraid she should laugh--' I never heard that a tom-turkey would set on eggs.'

"'Why, they ought to,' said the Parson getting quite 'arnest. 'What else be they good for? You just bring out the eggs, now, and put 'em in the nest, and I'll make him set on 'em.'

"So Huldy, she thought there weren't no way to convince him but to let him try; so she took the eggs out and fixed 'em all nice in the nest; and then she come back and found old Tom a-skirmishin' with the Parson pretty lively, I tell ye. Ye see, old Tom, he didn't take the idea at all; and he flopped and gobbled, and fit the Parson; and the Parson's wig got 'round so that his cue stuck straight out over his ear, but he'd got his blood up. Ye see, the old Doctor was used to carryin' his p'ints o' doctrine; and he hadn't fit the Arminians and Socinians to be beat by a tom-turkey; and finally he made a dive and ketched him by the neck in spite o' his floppin', and stroked him down, and put Huldy's apron 'round him.

"'There, Huldy,' he says, quite red in the face, 'we've got him now'; and he traveled off to the barn with him as lively as a cricket.

"Huldy came behind, just chokin' with laugh, and afraid the minister would look 'round and see her.

"'Now, Huldy, we'll crook his legs and set him down,' says the Parson, when they got him to the nest; 'you see, he is getting quiet, and he'll set there all right.'

"And the Parson, he sot him down; and old Tom, he sot there solemn enough and held his head down all droopin', lookin' like a rail pious old cock as long as the Parson sot by him.

"'There; you see how still he sets,' says the Parson to Huldy.

"Huldy was 'most dyin' for fear she should laugh. 'I'm afraid he'll get up,' says she, 'when you do.'

"'Oh, no, he won't!' says the Parson, quite confident. 'There, there,' says he, layin' his hands on him as if pronouncin' a blessin'.

"But when the Parson riz up, old Tom he riz up, too, and began to march over the eggs.

"'Stop, now!' says the Parson. 'I'll make him get down agin; hand me that corn-basket; we'll put that over him.'

"So he crooked old Tom's legs and got him down agin; and they put the corn-basket over him, and then they both stood and waited.

"'That'll do the thing, Huldy,' said the Parson.

"'I don't know about it,' says Huldy.

"'Oh, yes, it will, child; I understand,' says he.

"Just as he spoke, the basket riz up and stood, and they could see old Tom's long legs.

"'I'll make him stay down, confound him,' says the Parson, for you see, parsons is men, like the rest on us, and the Doctor had got his spunk up.

"'You jist hold him a minute, and I'll get something that'll make him stay, I guess; and out he went to the fence and brought in a long, thin, flat stone, and laid it on old Tom's back.

"'Oh, my eggs!' says Huldy. 'I'm afraid he's smashed 'em!'

"And sure enough, there they was, smashed flat enough under the stone.

"'I'll have him killed,' said the Parson. 'We won't have such a critter 'round.'

"Wall next week, Huldy, she jist borrowed the minister's horse and side-saddle and rode over to South Parish to her Aunt Bascome's-- Widder Bascome's, you know, that lives there by the trout-brook--and got a lot o' turkey eggs o' her, and come back and set a hen on 'em, and said nothin'; and in good time there was as nice a lot o' turkey- chicks as ever ye see.

"Huldy never said a word to the minister about his experiment, and he never said a word to her; but he sort o' kep more to his books and didn't take it on him to advise so much.

"But not long arter he took it into his head that Huldy ought to have a pig to be a-fattin' with the buttermilk.

"Mis' Pipperidge set him up to it; and jist then old Tom Bigelow, out to Juniper Hill, told him if he'd call over he'd give him a little pig.

"So he sent for a man, and told him to build a pig-pen right out by the well, and have it all ready when he came home with his pig.

"Huldy said she wished he might put a curb round the well out there, because in the dark sometimes a body might stumble into it; and the Parson said he might do that.

"Wal, old Aikin, the carpenter, he didn't come till 'most the middle of the afternoon; and then he sort o' idled, so that he didn't get up the well-curb till sun-down; and then he went off, and said he'd come and do the pig-pen next day.

"Wal, arter dark, Parson Carryl, he driv into the yard, full chizel, with his pig.

"'There, Huldy. I've got you a nice little pig.'

"'Dear me!' says Huldy; 'where have you put him?'

"'Why, out there in the pig-pen, to be sure.'

"'Oh, dear me!' says Huldy,'that's the well-curb--there ain't no pig- pen built,' says she.

"'Lordy massy!' says the Parson; 'then I've thrown the pig in the well!'

"Wal, Huldy she worked and worked, and finally she fished piggy out in the bucket, but he was as dead as a doornail; and she got him out o' the way quietly, and didn't say much; and the Parson he took to a great Hebrew book in his study.

"After that the Parson set sich store by Huldy that he come to her and asked her about everything, and it was amazin' how everything she put her hand to prospered. Huldy planted marigolds and larkspurs, pinks and carnations, all up and down the path to the front door; and trained up mornin'-glories and scarlet runners round the windows. And she was always gettin' a root here, and a sprig there, and a seed from somebody else; for Huldy was one o' them that has the gift, so that ef you jist give 'em the leastest of anything they make a great bush out of it right away; so that in six months Huldy had roses and geraniums and lilies sich as it would take a gardener to raise.

"Huldy was so sort o' chipper and fair spoken that she got the hired men all under her thumb: they come to her and took her orders jist as meek as so many calves, and she traded at the store, and kep' the accounts, and she had her eyes everywhere, and tied up all the ends so tight that there wa'n't no gettin' 'round her. She wouldn't let nobody put nothin' off on Parson Carryl 'cause he was a minister. Huldy was allers up to anybody that wanted to make a hard bargain, and afore he knew jist what he was about she'd got the best end of it, and everybody said that Huldy was the most capable girl they ever traded with.

"Wal, come to the meetin' of the Association, Mis' Deakin Blodgett and Mis' Pipperidge come callin' up to the Parson's all in a stew and offerin' their services to get the house ready, but the Doctor he jist thanked 'em quite quiet, and turned 'em over to Huldy; and Huldy she told 'em that she'd got everything ready, and showed 'em her pantries, and her cakes, and her pies, and her puddin's, and took 'em all over the house; and they went peekin' and pokin', openin' cupboard doors, and lookin' into drawers; and they couldn't find so much as a thread out o' the way, from garret to cellar, and so they went off quite discontented. Arter that the women sat a new trouble a-brewin'. They began to talk that it was a year now since Mis' Carryl died; and it railly wasn't proper such a young gal to be stayin' there, who everybody could see was a-settin' her cap for the minister.

"Mis' Pipperidge said, that so long as she looked on Huldy as the hired gal she hadn't thought much about it; but Huldy was railly takin' on airs as an equal, and appearin' as mistress o' the house in a way that would make talk if it went on. And Mis' Pipperidge she driv 'round up to Deakin Abner Snow's, and down to Mis 'Lijah Perry's, and asked them if they wasn't afraid that the way the Parson and Huldy was a-goin on might make talk. And they said they hadn't thought on't before, but now, come to think on't it, they was sure it would and they all went and talked with somebody else and asked them if they didn't think it would make talk. So come Sunday, between meetin's there warn't nothin' else talked about; and Huldy saw folks a-noddin' and a-winkin', and a-lookin' arter her, and she begun to feel drefful sort o' disagreeable. Finally Mis' Sawin, she says to her, 'My dear, didn't you never think folk would talk about you and the minister?'

"'No; why should they?' says Huldy, quite innocent.

"'Wal, dear,' says she, 'I think it's a shame; but they say you're tryin' to catch him, and that it's so bold and improper for you to be courtin' of him right in his own house--you know folks will talk--I thought I'd tell you, 'cause I think so much of you,' says she.

"Huldy was a gal of spirit, and she despised the talk, but it made her drefful uncomfortable; and when she got home at night she sat down in the mornin'-glory porch, quite quiet, and didn't sing a word.

"The minister he had heard the same thing from one of his deakins that day; and when he saw Huldy so kind o' silent, he says to her, 'Why don't you sing, my child?'

"He had a pleasant sort o' way with him, the minister had, and Huldy had got to likin' to be with him; and it all come over her that perhaps she ought to go away; and her throat kind o' filled up so she couldn't hardly speak; and, says she, 'I can't sing to-night'

"Says he, 'You don't know how much good your singin' has done me, nor how much good you have done me in all ways, Huldy. I wish I knew how to show my gratitude.'

"'Oh, sir!' says Huldy, 'is it improper for me to be here?'

"'No, dear,' says the minister, 'but ill-natured folks will talk; but there is one way we can stop it, Huldy--if you'll marry me. You'll make me very happy, and I'll do all I can to make you happy. Will you?'

"Wal, Huldy never told me just what she said to the minister; gals never does give you the particulars of them things jist as you'd like 'em--only I know the up-shot and the hull on't was, that Huldy she did a considerable lot o' clear starchin' and ironin' the next two days, and the Friday o' next week the minister and she rode over together to Doctor Lothrop's, in Oldtown, and the Doctor he jist made 'em man and wife."

William Dean Howells
MRS. JOHNSON

It was on a morning of the lovely New England May that we left the horse-car and, spreading our umbrellas, walked down the street to our new home in Charlesbridge, through a storm of snow and rain so finely blent by the influences of this fortunate climate that no flake knew itself from its sister drop, or could be better identified by the people against whom they beat in unison. A vernal gale from the east fanned our cheeks and pierced our marrow and chilled our blood, while the raw, cold green of the adventurous grass on the borders of the sopping sidewalks gave, as it peered through its veil of melting snow and freezing rain, a peculiar cheerfulness to the landscape. Here and there in the vacant lots abandoned hoopskirts defied decay; and near the half-finished wooden houses empty mortar-beds and bits of lath and slate, strewn over the scarred and mutilated ground, added their interest to the scene....

This heavenly weather, which the Pilgrim Fathers, with the idea of turning their thoughts effectually from earthly pleasures, came so far to discover, continued with slight amelioration throughout the month of May and far into June; and it was a matter of constant amazement with one who had known less austere climates, to behold how vegetable life struggled with the hostile skies, and, in an atmosphere as chill and damp as that of a cellar, shot forth the buds and blossoms upon the pear trees, called out the sour Puritan courage of the currant-bushes, taught a reckless native grapevine to wander and wanton over the southern side of the fence, and decked the banks with violets as fearless and as fragile as New England girls, so that about the end of June, when the heavens relented and the sun blazed out at last, there was little for him to do but to redden and darken the daring fruits that had attained almost their full growth without his countenance.

Then, indeed, Charlesbridge appeared to us a kind of paradise. The wind blew all day from the southwest, and all day in the grove across the way the orioles sang to their nestlings.... The house was almost new and in perfect repair; and, better than all, the kitchen had as yet given no signs of unrest in those volcanic agencies which are constantly at work there, and which, with sudden explosions, make Herculaneums and Pompeiis of so many smiling households. Breakfast, dinner and tea came up with illusive regularity, and were all the most perfect of their kind; and we laughed and feasted in our vain security. We had out from the city to banquet with us the friends we loved, and we were inexpressibly proud before them of the help who first wrought miracles of cookery in our honor, and then appeared in a clean white apron and the glossiest black hair to wait upon the table. She was young and certainly very pretty; she was as gay as a lark, and was courted by a young man whose clothes would have been a credit, if they had not been a reproach, to our lowly basement. She joyfully assented to the idea of staying with us till she married.

In fact, there was much that was extremely pleasant about the little place when the warm weather came, and it was not wonderful to us that Jenny was willing to remain. It was very quiet; we called one another to the window if a large dog went by our door; and whole days passed without the movement of any wheels but the butcher's upon our street, which flourished in ragweed and buttercups and daisies, and in the autumn burned, like the borders of nearly all the streets in Charlesbridge, with the pallid azure flame of the succory. The neighborhood was in all things a frontier between city and country. The horse-cars, the type of such civilization--full of imposture, discomfort, and sublime possibility--as we yet possess, went by the head of our street, and might, perhaps, be available to one skilled in calculating the movements of comets; while two minutes' walk would take us into a wood so wild and thick that no roof was visible through the trees. We learned, like innocent pastoral people of the golden age, to know the several voices of the cows pastured in the vacant lot, and, like engine-drivers of the iron-age, to distinguish the different whistles of the locomotives passing on the neighboring railroad. . . .

We played a little at gardening, of course, and planted tomatoes, which the chickens seemed to like, for they ate them up as fast as they ripened; and we watched with pride the growth of our Lawton blackberries, which, after attaining the most stalwart proportions, were still as bitter as the scrubbiest of their savage brethren, and which, when by advice left on the vines for a week after they turned black, were silently gorged by secret and gluttonous flocks of robins and orioles. As for our grapes, the frost cut them off in the hour of their triumph.

So, as I have hinted, we were not surprised that Jenny should be willing to remain with us, and were as little prepared for her desertion as for any other change of our mortal state. But one day in September she came to her nominal mistress with tears in her beautiful eyes and protestations of unexampled devotion upon her tongue, and said that she was afraid she must leave us. She liked the place, and she never had worked for anyone that was more of a lady, but she had made up her mind to go into the city. All this, so far, was quite in the manner of domestics who, in ghost stories, give warning to the occupants of haunted houses; and Jenny's mistress listened in suspense for the motive of her desertion, expecting to hear no less than that it was something which walked up and down the stairs and dragged iron links after it, or something that came and groaned at the front door, like populace dissatisfied with a political candidate. But it was in fact nothing of this kind; simply, there were no lamps upon our street, and Jenny, after spending Sunday evenings with friends in East Charlesbridge, was always alarmed on her return in walking from the horse-car to our door. The case was hopeless, and Jenny and our household parted with respect and regret.

We had not before this thought it a grave disadvantage that our street was unlighted. Our street was not drained nor graded; no municipal cart ever came to carry away our ashes; there was not a water-butt within half a mile to save us from fire, nor more than the one-thousandth part of a policeman to protect us from theft. Yet, as I paid a heavy tax, I somehow felt that we enjoyed the benefits of city government, and never looked upon Charlesbridge as in any way undesirable for residence. But when it became necessary to find help in Jenny's place, the frosty welcome given to application at the intelligence offices renewed a painful doubt awakened by her departure. To be sure, the heads of the offices were polite enough; but when the young housekeeper had stated her case at the first to which she applied, and the Intelligencer had called out to the invisible expectants in the adjoining room, "Anny wan wants to do giner'l housewark in Charlsbrudge?" there came from the maids invoked so loud, so fierce, so full a "No!" as shook the lady's heart with an indescribable shame and dread. The name that, with an innocent pride in its literary and historical associations, she had written at the heads of her letters, was suddenly become a matter of reproach to her; and she was almost tempted to conceal thereafter that she lived in Charlesbridge, and to pretend that she dwelt upon some wretched little street in Boston. "You see," said the head of the office, "the gairls doesn't like to live so far away from the city. Now, if it was on'y in the Port." ...

This pen is not graphic enough to give the remote reader an idea of the affront offered to an inhabitant of Old Charlesbridge in these closing words. Neither am I of sufficiently tragic mood to report here all the sufferings undergone by an unhappy family in finding servants, or to tell how the winter was passed with miserable makeshifts. Alas! is it not the history of a thousand experiences? Anyone who looks upon this page could match it with a tale as full of heartbreak and disaster, while I conceive that, in hastening to speak of Mrs. Johnson, I approach a subject of unique interest. ...

I say our last Irish girl went with the last snow, and on one of those midsummerlike days that sometimes fall in early April to our yet bleak and desolate zone, our hearts sang of Africa and golden joys. A Libyan longing took us, and we would have chosen, if we could, to bear a strand of grotesque beads, or a handful of brazen gauds, and traffic them for some sable maid with crisp locks, whom, uncoffling from the captive train beside the desert, we should make to do our general housework forever, through the right of lawful purchase. But we knew that this was impossible, and that if we desired colored help we must seek it at the intelligence office, which is in one of those streets chiefly inhabited by the orphaned children and grandchildren of slavery. To tell the truth, these orphans do not seem to grieve much for their bereavement, but lead a life of joyous and rather indolent oblivion in their quarter of the city. They are often to be seen sauntering up and down the street by which the Oharlesbridge cars arrive--the young with a harmless swagger and the old with the generic limp which our Autocrat has already noted as attending advanced years in their race.... How gaily are the young ladies of this race attired, as they trip up and down the sidewalks, and in and out through the pendant garments at the shop doors! They are the black pansies and marigolds, and dark- blooded dahlias among womankind. They try to assume something of our colder race's demeanor, but even the passer on the horse-car can see that it is not native with them, and is better pleased when they forget us, and ungenteely laugh in encountering friends, letting their white teeth glitter through the generous lips that open to their ears. In the streets branching upward from this avenue, very little colored men and maids play with broken or enfeebled toys, or sport on the wooden pavements of the entrances to the inner courts. Now and then a colored soldier or sailor--looking strange in his uniform even after the custom of several years--emerges f rom those passages; or, more rarely, a black gentleman, stricken in years, and cased in shining broadcloth, walks solidly down the brick sidewalk, cane in hand--a vision of serene self-complacency and so plainly the expression of virtuous public sentiment that the great colored louts, innocent enough till then in their idleness, are taken with a sudden sense of depravity, and loaf guiltily up against the house-walls. At the same moment, perhaps, a young damsel, amorously scuffling with an admirer through one of the low open windows, suspends the strife, and bids him--"Go along, now, do!" More rarely yet than the gentleman described, one may see a white girl among the dark neighbors, whose frowsy head is uncovered, and whose sleeves are rolled up to her elbows, and who, though no doubt quite at home, looks as strange there as that pale anomaly which may sometimes be seen among a crew of blackbirds.

An air not so much of decay as of unthrift, and yet hardly of unthrift, seems to prevail in the neighborhood, which has none of the aggressive and impudent squalor of an Irish quarter and none of the surly wickedenss of a low American street. A gaiety not born of the things that bring its serious joy to the true New England heart--a ragged gaiety, which comes of summer in the blood, and not in the pocket or the conscience, and which affects the countenance and the whole demeanor, setting the feet to some inward music, and at times bursting into a line of song or a childlike and irresponsible laugh-- gives tone to the visible life and wakens a very friendly spirit in the passer, who somehow thinks there of a milder climate, and is half persuaded that the orange-peel on the sidewalks came from fruit grown in the soft atmosphere of those back courts.

It was in this quarter, then, that we heard of Mrs. Johnson; and it was from a colored boarding-house there that she came to Charlesbridge to look at us, bringing her daughter of twelve years with her. She was a matron of mature age and portly figure, with a complexion like coffee soothed with the richest cream; and her manners were so full of a certain tranquillity and grace that she charmed away all our will to ask for references. It was only her barbaric laughter and lawless eye that betrayed how slightly her New England birth and breeding covered her ancestral traits, and bridged the gulf of a thousand years of civilization that lay between her race and ours. But in fact, she was doubly estranged by descent; for, as we learned later, a sylvan wilderness mixed with that of the desert in her veins; her grandfather was an Indian, and her ancestors on this side had probably sold their lands for the same value in trinkets that bought the original African pair on the other side.

The first day that Mrs. Johnson descended into our kitchen she conjured from the malicious disorder in which it had been left by the flitting Irish kobold a dinner that revealed the inspirations of genius, and was quite different from a dinner of mere routine and laborious talent. Something original and authentic mingled with the accustomed flavors; and, though vague reminiscences of canal-boat travel and woodland camps arose from the relish of certain of the dishes, there was yet the assurance of such power in the preparation of the whole that we knew her to be merely running over the chords of our appetite with preliminary savors, as a musician acquaints his touch with the keys of an unfamiliar piano before breaking into brilliant and triumphant execution. Within a week she had mastered her instrument, and thereafter there was no faltering in her performances, which she varied constantly, through inspiration or from suggestion.... But, after all, it was in puddings that Mrs. Johnson chiefly excelled. She was one of those cooks--rare as men of genius in literature--who love their own dishes; and she had, in her personally childlike simplicity of taste and the inherited appetites of her savage forefathers, a dominant passion for sweets. So far as we could learn, she subsisted principally upon puddings and tea. Through the same primitive instincts, no doubt, she loved praise. She openly exulted in our artless flatteries of her skill; she waited jealously at the head of the kitchen stairs to hear what was said of her work, especially if there were guests; and she was never too weary to attempt emprises of cookery.

While engaged in these, she wore a species of sightly handkerchief like a turban upon her head, and about her person those mystical swathings in which old ladies of the African race delight. But she most pleasured our sense of beauty and moral fitness when, after the last pan was washed and the last pot was scraped, she lighted a potent pipe, and, taking her stand at the kitchen door, laded the soft evening air with its pungent odors. If we surprised her at these supreme moments, she took the pipe from her lips and put it behind her, with a low, mellow chuckle and a look of half-defiant consciousness, never guessing that none of her merits took us half so much as the cheerful vice which she only feigned to conceal.

Some things she could not do so perfectly as cooking because of her failing eyesight, and we persuaded her that spectacles would both become and befriend a lady of her years, and so bought her a pair of steel-bowed glasses. She wore them in some great emergencies at first, but had clearly no pride in them. Before long she laid them aside altogether, and they had passed from our thoughts, when one day we heard her mellow note of laughter and her daughter's harsher cackle outside our door, and, opening it, beheld Mrs. Johnson in gold-bowed spectacles of massive frame. We then learned that their purchase was in fulfilment of a vow made long ago, in the lifetime of Mr. Johnson, that if ever she wore glasses, they should be gold- bowed; and I hope the manes of the dead were half as happy in these votive spectacles as the simple soul that offered them.

She and her late partner were the parents of eleven children, some of whom were dead and some of whom were wanderers in unknown parts. During his lifetime she had kept a little shop in her native town, and it was only within a few years that she had gone into service. She cherished a natural haughtiness of spirit, and resented control, although disposed to do all she could of her own notion. Being told to say when she wanted an afternoon, she explained that when she wanted an afternoon she always took it without asking, but always planned so as not to discommode the ladies with whom she lived. These, she said, had numbered twenty-seven within three years, which made us doubt the success of her system in all cases, though she merely held out the fact as an assurance of her faith in the future, and a proof of the ease with which places are to be found. She contended, moreover, that a lady who had for thirty years had a house of her own was in nowise bound to ask permission to receive visits from friends where she might be living, but that they ought freely to come and go like other guests. In this spirit she once invited her son-in-law, Professor Jones, of Providence, to dine with her; and her defied mistress, on entering the dining-room found the Professor at pudding and tea there-- an impressively respectable figure in black clothes, with a black face rendered yet more effective by a pair of green goggles. It appeared that this dark professor was a light of phrenology in Rhode Island, and that he was believed to have uncommon virtue in his science by reason of being blind as well as black.

I am loath to confess that Mrs. Johnson had not a flattering opinion of the Caucasian race in all respects. In fact, she had very good philosophical and scriptural reasons for looking upon us as an upstart people of new blood, who had come into their whiteness by no creditable or pleasant process. The late Mr. Johnson, who had died in the West Indies, whither he voyaged for his health in quality of a cook upon a Down East schooner, was a man of letters, and had written a book to show the superiority of the black over the white branches of the human family. In this he held that, as all islands have been at their first discovery found peopled by blacks, we must needs believe that humanity was first created of that color. Mrs. Johnson could not show us her husband's work (a sole copy in the library of an English gentleman at Port au Prince is not to be bought for money), but she often developed its arguments to the lady of the house; and one day, with a great show of reluctance and many protests that no personal slight was meant, let fall the fact that Mr. Johnson believed the white race descended from Gehaz the leper, upon whom the leprosy of Naaman fell when the latter returned by divine favor to his original blackness. "And he went out from his presence a leper as white as snow," said Mrs. Johnson, quoting irrefutable Scripture. "Leprosy, leprosy," she added thoughtfully--"nothing but leprosy bleached you out."

It seems to me much in her praise that she did not exult in our taint and degradation, as some white philosophers used to do in the opposite idea that a part of the human family were cursed to lasting blackness and slavery in Ham and his children, but even told us of a remarkable approach to whiteness in many of her own offspring. In a kindred spirit of charity, no doubt, she refused ever to attend church with people of her elder and wholesomer blood. When she went to church, she said, she always went to a white church, though while with us I am bound to say she never went to any. She professed to read her Bible in her bedroom on Sundays; but we suspected from certain sounds and odors which used to steal out of this sanctuary, that her piety more commonly found expression in dozing and smoking.

I would not make a wanton jest here of Mrs. Johnson's anxiety to claim honor for the African color, while denying this color in many of her own family. It afforded a glimpse of the pain with which all her people must endure, however proudly they hide it or light- heartedly forget it, from the despite and contumely to which they are guiltlessly born; and when I thought how irreparable was this disgrace and calamity of a black skin, and how irreparable it must be for ages yet, in this world where every other chance and all manner of wilful guilt and wickedness may hope for covert and pardon, I had little heart to laugh. Indeed, it was so pathetic to hear this poor old soul talk of her dead and lost ones, and try, in spite of all Mr. Johnson's theories and her own arrogant generalizations to establish their whiteness, that we must have been very cruel and silly people to turn their sacred fables even into matter of question. I have no doubt that her Antoinette Anastasia and her Thomas Jefferson Wilberforce--it is impossible to give a full idea of the splendor and scope of the baptismal names in Mrs. Johnson's family--have as light skins and as golden hair in heaven as her reverend maternal fancy painted for them in our world. There, certainly, they would not be subject to tanning, which had ruined the delicate complexion, and had knotted into black woolly tangles the once wavy blond locks of our little maid-servant Naomi; and I would fain believe that Toussaint Washington Johnson, who ran away to sea so many years ago, has found some fortunate zone where his hair and skin keep the same sunny and rosy tints they wore to his mother's eyes in infancy. But I have no means of knowing this, or of telling whether he was the prodigy of intellect that he was declared to be. Naomi could no more be taken in proof of the one assertion than of the other. When she came to us, it was agreed that she should go to school; but she overruled her mother in this as in everything else, and never went. Except Sunday-school lessons, she had no other instructions than that her mistress gave her in the evenings, when a heavy day's play and the natural influences of the hour conspired with original causes to render her powerless before words of one syllable.

The first week of her services she was obedient and faithful to her duties; but, relaxing in the atmosphere of a house which seems to demoralize all menials, she shortly fell into disorderly ways of lying in wait for callers out of doors, and, when people rang, of running up the front steps and letting them in from the outside. As the season expanded, and the fine weather became confirmed, she spent her time in the fields, appearing at the house only when nature importunately craved molasses.

In her untamable disobedience, Naomi alone betrayed her sylvan blood, for she was in all other respects Negro and not Indian. But it was of her aboriginal ancestry that Mrs. Johnson chiefly boasted--when not engaged in argument to maintain the superiority of the African race. She loved to descant upon it as the cause and explanation of her own arrogant habit of feeling; and she seemed, indeed, to have inherited something of the Indian's *hauteur* along with the Ethiop's subtle cunning and abundant amiability. She gave many instances in which her pride had met and overcome the insolence of employers, and the kindly old creature was by no means singular in her pride of being reputed proud.

She could never have been a woman of strong logical faculties, but she had in some things a very surprising and awful astuteness. She seldom introduced any purpose directly, but bore all about it, and then suddenly sprung it upon her unprepared antagonist. At other times she obscurely hinted a reason, and left a conclusion to be inferred; as when she warded off reproach for some delinquency by saying in a general way that she had lived with ladies who used to come scolding into the kitchen after they had taken their bitters. "Quality ladies took their bitters regular," she added, to remove any sting of personality from her remark; for, from many things she had let fall, we knew that she did not regard us as quality. On the contrary, she often tried to overbear us with the gentility of her former places; and would tell the lady over whom she reigned that she had lived with folks worth their three and four hundred thousand dollars, who never complained as she did of the ironing. Yet she had a sufficient regard for the literary occupations of the family, Mr. Johnson having been an author. She even professed to have herself written a book, which was still in manuscript and preserved somewhere among her best clothes.

It was well, on many accounts, to be in contact with a mind so original and suggestive as Mrs. Johnson's. We loved to trace its intricate yet often transparent operations, and were perhaps too fond of explaining its peculiarities by facts of ancestry--of finding hints of the Pow-wow of the Grand Custom in each grotesque development. We were conscious of something warmer in this old soul than in ourselves, and sometimes wilder, and we chose to think it the tropic and the untracked forest. She had scarcely any being apart from her affection; she had no morality, but was good because she neither hated nor envied; and she might have been a saint far more easily than far more civilized people.

There was that also in her sinuous yet malleable nature, so full of guile and so full of goodness, that reminded us pleasantly of lowly folks in elder lands, where relaxing oppressions have lifted the restraints of fear between master and servant without disturbing the familiarity of their relation. She advised freely with us upon all household matters, and took a motherly interest in whatever concerned us. She could be flattered or caressed into almost any service, but no threat or command could move her. When she erred, she never acknowledged her wrong in words, but handsomely expressed her regrets in a pudding or sent up her apologies in a favorite dish secretly prepared. We grew so well used to this form of exculpation that, whenever Mrs. Johnson took an afternoon at an inconvenient season, we knew that for a week afterward we should be feasted like princes. She owned frankly that she loved us, that she never had done half so much for people before, and that she never had been nearly so well suited in any other place; and for a brief and happy time we thought that we never should be obliged to part.

One day, however, our dividing destiny appeared in the basement, and was presented to us as Hippolyto Thucydides, the son of Mrs. Johnson, who had just arrived on a visit to his mother from the State of New Hampshire. He was a heavy and loutish youth, standing upon the borders of boyhood, and looking forward to the future with a vacant and listless eye. I mean this was his figurative attitude; his actual manner, as he lolled upon a chair beside the kitchen window, was so eccentric that we felt a little uncertain how to regard him, and Mrs. Johnson openly described him as peculiar. He was so deeply tanned by the fervid suns of the New Hampshire winter, and his hair had so far suffered from the example of the sheep lately under his charge, that he could not be classed by any stretch of compassion with the blond and straight-haired members of Mrs. Johnson's family.

He remained with us all the first day until late in the afternoon, when his mother took him out to get him a boarding-house. Then he departed in the van of her and Naomi, pausing at the gate to collect his spirits, and, after he had sufficiently animated himself by clapping his palms together, starting off down the street at a hand- gallop, to the manifest terror of the cows in the pasture and the confusion of the less demonstrative people of our household. Other characteristic traits appeared in Hippolyto Thucydides within no very long period of time, and he ran away from his lodgings so often during the summer that he might be said to board round among the outlying cornfields and turnip patches of Charlesbridge. As a check upon this habit, Mrs. Johnson seemed to have invited him to spend his whole time in our basement; for whenever we went below we found him there, balanced--perhaps in homage to us, and perhaps as a token of extreme sensibility in himself--upon the low window-sill, the bottoms of his boots touching the floor inside, and his face buried in the grass without.

We could formulate no very tenable objection to all this, and yet the presence of Thucydides in our kitchen unaccountably oppressed our imaginations. We beheld him all over the house, a monstrous eidolon, balanced upon every window-sill; and he certainly attracted unpleasant notice to our place, no less by his furtive and hang-dog manner of arrival than by the bold displays with which he celebrated his departures. We hinted this to Mrs. Johnson, but she could not enter into our feeling. Indeed, all the wild poetry of her maternal and primitive nature seemed to cast itself about this hapless boy; and if we had listened to her we should have believed that there was no one so agreeable in society, or so quickwitted in affairs, as Hippolyto, when he chose. ...

At last, when we said positively that Thucydides should come to us no more, and then qualified the prohibition by allowing him to come every Sunday, she answered that she never would hurt the child's feelings by telling him not to come where his mother was; that people who did not love her children did not love her; and that, if Hippy went, she went. We thought it a masterpiece of firmness to rejoin that Hippolyto must go in any event, but I am bound to own that he did not go, and that his mother stayed, and so fed us with every cunning, propitiatory dainty, that we must have been Pagans to renew our threat. In fact, we begged Mrs. Johnson to go into the country with us, and she, after long reluctation on Hippy's account, consented, agreeing to send him away to friends during her absence.

We made every preparation, and on the eve of our departure Mrs. Johnson went into the city to engage her son's passage to Bangor, while we awaited her return in untroubled security.

But she did not appear until midnight, and then responded with but a sad "Well, sah!" to the cheerful "Well, Mrs. Johnson!" that greeted her.

"All right, Mrs. Johnson?"

Mrs. Johnson made a strange noise, half chuckle and half death-rattle in her throat. "All wrong, sah. Hippy's off again; and I've been all over the city after him."

"Then you can't go with us in the morning?"

"How *can* I, sah?"

Mrs. Johnson went sadly out of the room. Then she came back to the door again, and opening it, uttered, for the first time in our service, words of apology and regret: "I hope I ha'n't put you out any. I *wanted* to go with you, but I ought to *knowed* I couldn't. All is, I loved you too much."--Suburban Sketches.

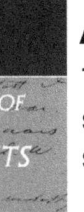

The Codes Of Hammurabi And Moses
W. W. Davies

QTY

The discovery of the Hammurabi Code is one of the greatest achievements of archaeology, and is of paramount interest, not only to the student of the Bible, but also to all those interested in ancient history...

Religion   ISBN: *1-59462-338-4*   **Pages:132**

MSRP $12.95

The Theory of Moral Sentiments
Adam Smith

QTY

This work from 1749. contains original theories of conscience amd moral judgment and it is the foundation for systemof morals.

Philosophy ISBN: *1-59462-777-0*   **Pages:536**

MSRP $19.95

Jessica's First Prayer
Hesba Stretton

QTY

In a screened and secluded corner of one of the many railway-bridges which span the streets of London there could be seen a few years ago, from five o'clock every morning until half past eight, a tidily set-out coffee-stall, consisting of a trestle and board, upon which stood two large tin cans, with a small fire of charcoal burning under each so as to keep the coffee boiling during the early hours of the morning when the work-people were thronging into the city on their way to their daily toil...

Pages:84

Childrens   ISBN: *1-59462-373-2*   *MSRP $9.95*

My Life and Work
Henry Ford

QTY

Henry Ford revolutionized the world with his implementation of mass production for the Model T automobile. Gain valuable business insight into his life and work with his own auto-biography... "We have only started on our development of our country we have not as yet, with all our talk of wonderful progress, done more than scratch the surface. The progress has been wonderful enough but..."

Pages:300

Biographies/   ISBN: *1-59462-198-5*   *MSRP $21.95*

The Art of Cross-Examination
Francis Wellman

QTY

I presume it is the experience of every author, after his first book is published upon an important subject, to be almost overwhelmed with a wealth of ideas and illustrations which could readily have been included in his book, and which to his own mind, at least, seem to make a second edition inevitable. Such certainly was the case with me; and when the first edition had reached its sixth impression in five months, I rejoiced to learn that it seemed to my publishers that the book had met with a sufficiently favorable reception to justify a second and considerably enlarged edition. ..

Reference   ISBN: *1-59462-647-2*

Pages:412

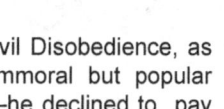

MSRP $19.95

On the Duty of Civil Disobedience
Henry David Thoreau

QTY

Thoreau wrote his famous essay, On the Duty of Civil Disobedience, as a protest against an unjust but popular war and the immoral but popular institution of slave-owning. He did more than write—he declined to pay his taxes, and was hauled off to gaol in consequence. Who can say how much this refusal of his hastened the end of the war and of slavery ?

Law   ISBN: *1-59462-747-9*

Pages:48

MSRP $7.45

Dream Psychology Psychoanalysis for Beginners
Sigmund Freud

QTY

Sigmund Freud, born Sigismund Schlomo Freud (May 6, 1856 - September 23, 1939), was a Jewish-Austrian neurologist and psychiatrist who co-founded the psychoanalytic school of psychology. Freud is best known for his theories of the unconscious mind, especially involving the mechanism of repression; his redefinition of sexual desire as mobile and directed towards a wide variety of objects; and his therapeutic techniques, especially his understanding of transference in the therapeutic relationship and the presumed value of dreams as sources of insight into unconscious desires.

Dream Psychology
Psychoanalysis for Beginners

Sigmund Freud

Psychology   ISBN: *1-59462-905-6*

Pages:196

MSRP $15.45

The Miracle of Right Thought
Orison Swett Marden

QTY

Believe with all of your heart that you will do what you were made to do. When the mind has once formed the habit of holding cheerful, happy, prosperous pictures, it will not be easy to form the opposite habit. It does not matter how improbable or how far away this realization may see, or how dark the prospects may be, if we visualize them as best we can, as vividly as possible, hold tenaciously to them and vigorously struggle to attain them, they will gradually become actualized, realized in the life. But a desire, a longing without endeavor, a yearning abandoned or held indifferently will vanish without realization.

Self Help   ISBN: *1-59462-644-8*

Pages:360

MSRP $25.45

The Rosicrucian Cosmo-Conception Mystic Christianity *by Max Heindel* ISBN: *1-59462-188-8* **$38.95**
The Rosicrucian Cosmo-conception is not dogmatic, neither does it appeal to any other authority than the reason of the student. It is: not controversial, but is: sent forth in the, hope that it may help to clear... New Age/Religion Pages 646

Abandonment To Divine Providence *by Jean-Pierre de Caussade* ISBN: *1-59462-228-0* **$25.95**
"The Rev. Jean Pierre de Caussade was one of the most remarkable spiritual writers of the Society of Jesus in France in the 18th Century. His death took place at Toulouse in 1751. His works have gone through many editions and have been republished... Inspirational/Religion Pages 400

Mental Chemistry *by Charles Haanel* ISBN: *1-59462-192-6* **$23.95**
Mental Chemistry allows the change of material conditions by combining and appropriately utilizing the power of the mind. Much like applied chemistry creates something new and unique out of careful combinations of chemicals the mastery of mental chemistry... New Age Pages 354

The Letters of Robert Browning and Elizabeth Barret Barrett 1845-1846 vol II ISBN: *1-59462-193-4* **$35.95**
by Robert Browning and Elizabeth Barrett Biographies Pages 596

Gleanings In Genesis (volume I) *by Arthur W. Pink* ISBN: *1-59462-130-6* **$27.45**
Appropriately has Genesis been termed "the seed plot of the Bible" for in it we have, in germ form, almost all of the great doctrines which are afterwards fully developed in the books of Scripture which follow... Religion/Inspirational Pages 420

The Master Key *by L. W. de Laurence* ISBN: *1-59462-001-6* **$30.95**
In no branch of human knowledge has there been a more lively increase of the spirit of research during the past few years than in the study of Psychology, Concentration and Mental Discipline. The requests for authentic lessons in Thought Control, Mental Discipline and... New Age/Business Pages 422

The Lesser Key Of Solomon Goetia *by L. W. de Laurence* ISBN: *1-59462-092-X* **$9.95**
This translation of the first book of the "Lernegton" which is now for the first time made accessible to students of Talismanic Magic was done, after careful collation and edition, from numerous Ancient Manuscripts in Hebrew, Latin, and French... New Age/Occult Pages 92

Rubaiyat Of Omar Khayyam *by Edward Fitzgerald* ISBN:*1-59462-332-5* **$13.95**
Edward Fitzgerald, whom the world has already learned, in spite of his own efforts to remain within the shadow of anonymity, to look upon as one of the rarest poets of the century, was born at Bredfield, in Suffolk, on the 31st of March, 1809. He was the third son of John Purcell... Music Pages 172

Ancient Law *by Henry Maine* ISBN: *1-59462-128-4* **$29.95**
The chief object of the following pages is to indicate some of the earliest ideas of mankind, as they are reflected in Ancient Law, and to point out the relation of those ideas to modern thought. Religiom/History Pages 452

Far-Away Stories *by William J. Locke* ISBN: *1-59462-129-2* **$19.45**
"Good wine needs no bush, but a collection of mixed vintages does. And this book is just such a collection. Some of the stories I do not want to remain buried for ever in the museum files of dead magazine-numbers an author's not unpardonable vanity..." Fiction Pages 272

Life of David Crockett *by David Crockett* ISBN: *1-59462-250-7* **$27.45**
"Colonel David Crockett was one of the most remarkable men of the times in which he lived. Born in humble life, but gifted with a strong will, an indomitable courage, and unremitting perseverance... Biographies/New Age Pages 424

Lip-Reading *by Edward Nitchie* ISBN: *1-59462-206-X* **$25.95**
Edward B. Nitchie, founder of the New York School for the Hard of Hearing, now the Nitchie School of Lip-Reading, Inc, wrote "LIP-READING Principles and Practice". The development and perfecting of this meritorious work on lip-reading was an undertaking... How-to Pages 400

A Handbook of Suggestive Therapeutics, Applied Hypnotism, Psychic Science ISBN: *1-59462-214-0* **$24.95**
by Henry Munro Health/New Age/Health/Self-help Pages 376

A Doll's House: and Two Other Plays *by Henrik Ibsen* ISBN: *1-59462-112-8* **$19.95**
Henrik Ibsen created this classic when in revolutionary 1848 Rome. Introducing some striking concepts in playwriting for the realist genre, this play has been studied the world over. Fiction/Classics/Plays 308

The Light of Asia *by sir Edwin Arnold* ISBN: *1-59462-204-3* **$13.95**
In this poetic masterpiece, Edwin Arnold describes the life and teachings of Buddha. The man who was to become known as Buddha to the world was born as Prince Gautama of India but he rejected the worldly riches and abandoned the reigns of power when... Religion/History/Biographies Pages 170

The Complete Works of Guy de Maupassant *by Guy de Maupassant* ISBN: *1-59462-157-8* **$16.95**
"For days and days, nights and nights, I had dreamed of that first kiss which was to consecrate our engagement, and I knew not on what spot I should put my lips..." Fiction/Classics Pages 240

The Art of Cross-Examination *by Francis L. Wellman* ISBN: *1-59462-309-0* **$26.95**
Written by a renowned trial lawyer, Wellman imparts his experience and uses case studies to explain how to use psychology to extract desired information through questioning. How-to/Science/Reference Pages 408

Answered or Unanswered? *by Louisa Vaughan* ISBN: *1-59462-248-5* **$10.95**
Miracles of Faith in China Religion Pages 112

The Edinburgh Lectures on Mental Science (1909) *by Thomas* ISBN: *1-59462-008-3* **$11.95**
This book contains the substance of a course of lectures recently given by the writer in the Queen Street Hall, Edinburgh. Its purpose is to indicate the Natural Principles governing the relation between Mental Action and Material Conditions... New Age/Psychology Pages 148

Ayesha *by H. Rider Haggard* ISBN: *1-59462-301-5* **$24.95**
Verily and indeed it is the unexpected that happens! Probably if there was one person upon the earth from whom the Editor of this, and of a certain previous history, did not expect to hear again... Classics Pages 380

Ayala's Angel *by Anthony Trollope* ISBN: *1-59462-352-X* **$29.95**
The two girls were both pretty, but Lucy who was twenty-one who supposed to be simple and comparatively unattractive, whereas Ayala was credited, as her Bombwhat romantic name might show, with poetic charm and a taste for romance. Ayala when her father died was nineteen... Fiction Pages 484

The American Commonwealth *by James Bryce* ISBN: *1-59462-286-8* **$34.45**
An interpretation of American democratic political theory. It examines political mechanics and society from the perspective of Scotsman James Bryce Politics Pages 572

Stories of the Pilgrims *by Margaret P. Pumphrey* ISBN: *1-59462-116-0* **$17.95**
This book explores pilgrims religious oppression in England as well as their escape to Holland and eventual crossing to America on the Mayflower, and their early days in New England... History Pages 268

QTY

The Fasting Cure *by Sinclair Upton*   ISBN: *1-59462-222-1*   **$13.95**
In the Cosmopolitan Magazine for May, 1910, and in the Contemporary Review (London) for April, 1910, I published an article dealing with my experi-ences in fasting. I have written a great many magazine articles, but never one which attracted so much attention... New Age/Self Help/Health Pages 164

Hebrew Astrology *by Sepharial*   ISBN: *1-59462-308-2*   **$13.45**
In these days of advanced thinking it is a matter of common observation that we have left many of the old landmarks behind and that we are now pressing forward to greater heights and to a wider horizon than that which represented the mind-content of our progenitors...   Astrology Pages 144

Thought Vibration or The Law of Attraction in the Thought World   ISBN: *1-59462-127-6*   **$12.95**

by William Walker Atkinson   *Psychology/Religion Pages 144*

Optimism *by Helen Keller*   ISBN: *1-59462-108-X*   **$15.95**
Helen Keller was blind, deaf, and mute since 19 months old, yet famously learned how to overcome these handicaps, communicate with the world, and spread her lectures promoting optimism. An inspiring read for everyone...   Biographies/Inspirational Pages 84

Sara Crewe *by Frances Burnett*   ISBN: *1-59462-360-0*   **$9.45**
In the first place, Miss Minchin lived in London. Her home was a large, dull, tall one, in a large, dull square, where all the houses were alike, and all the sparrows were alike, and where all the door-knockers made the same heavy sound...   Childrens/Classic Pages 88

The Autobiography of Benjamin Franklin *by Benjamin Franklin*   ISBN: *1-59462-135-7*   **$24.95**
The Autobiography of Benjamin Franklin has probably been more extensively read than any other American historical work, and no other book of its kind has had such ups and downs of fortune. Franklin lived for many years in England, where he was agent...   Biographies/History Pages 332

Name	
Email	
Telephone	
Address	
City, State ZIP	

☐ **Credit Card**   ☐ **Check / Money Order**

Credit Card Number	
Expiration Date	
Signature	

Please Mail to: Book Jungle
PO Box 2226
Champaign, IL 61825
or Fax to: 630-214-0564

www.ingramcontent.com/pod-product-compliance
Lightning Source LLC
Chambersburg PA
CBHW080745250626
47162CB00010B/3033